Brain:

The Man Who Wrote the Book That Changed the World

by Dermot Davis

Most Expression Unleashed Publishing (eXu) print books are available at special quantity bulk purchase discounts for promotional, education or other needs. Additionally, special book excerpts may be created for unique projects. For details, contact the publisher.

Expression Unleashed Publishing, Los Angeles, California
http://expressionunleashed.com

Dermot Davis (2013-7-04). *Brain: The Man Who Wrote the Book That Changed the World.* Expression Unleashed Publishing. Print, 1st Edition. Printed in the United States of America.

ISBN: 0-9844181-3-X
ISBN-13: 978-0-9844181-3-8

DEDICATION

For Darby Shields,
a true patron of the arts.

CONTENTS

PROLOGUE

It was graduation day at the University of Tollston in Illinois. Before the assembled students and their families, Dean Reynolds stood at the podium to announce the recipient of the prestigious Marcus and Imelda Rogerspoon award for the student showing the brightest promise for a future literary career.

Although the majority of the persons in attendance didn't give a whit about the prestigious award, or who that year's recipient might be, the handful of literary types present knew that it was short-listed to just two people: the intense intellectual, Daniel Waterstone and the artsy, anti-establishment, outspoken radical, "Crazy" Mary McIntyre.

The Dean spoke into the microphone, the incorrect placement of speakers producing a faint echoing effect. "Founder of the campus publication, *Superior Review,* and the student deemed to be most likely to succeed in the art of story-telling, the award goes to... Daniel Waterstone."

Daniel jumped to his feet with glee and was only half successful in suppressing his impulse to punch the air with a clenched fist. He energetically shook the hands of several disinterested students, who just happened to be sitting in his row, and made his way to the raised platform. Perhaps, in his head, he equated being the recipient of this obscure award with winning an Oscar, so, to the accompaniment of very modest applause, he summarily shook the hand of each of the male faculty and kissed the cheeks of each of the indifferent females he met on his way to the podium.

He then bear-hugged the impatient dean who did not see the hug coming and who subsequently failed, in an awkward way, to complete the hug from his end. Beaming with pride and self-confidence, Daniel received the award in his left hand whilst vigorously pumping the Dean's hand with his right. Expecting Daniel to return to his seat, the Dean replaced his reading glasses and checked his notes to move on to whatever was next on the agenda.

Daniel, however, was not about to let his five seconds of minor fame conclude so quickly and so he proceeded to pull out, from an inside pocket, what appeared to be a prepared speech. Adjusting the microphone to his desired height, Daniel addressed what was now a puzzled and somewhat bemused audience.

"Dean, members of the staff, ladies and gentlemen, it is with tremendous pride and heartfelt honor that I accept this highly-esteemed and influential award," he began and then looked around to make sure he had everyone's attention.

"We are living in dangerous times," he then said, pausing, for dramatic effect. "Having progressed through the age of reason and enlightenment, civilization is now poised to enter the age of insanity. I tell you, in no uncertain terms that what we are currently witnessing, at least here, in the West, is the decline of culture itself."

Whereas the academically inclined did perk up somewhat to these stark revelations, the majority of the persons in attendance were mentally preoccupied and paid his words of doom no heed. "We live in a time, reminiscent of the declining Roman Empire, perhaps, where style is rewarded over content and where worthy conversation concerning the evolution of our culture is replaced with inconsequential nonsense such as gossip about the lifestyles of the rich and famous. Our literature has been in decline for decades. Loopy fads and fantasy genres, of questionable merit, now clog our once-great literary arteries."

As many in the audience took this opportunity to pay a much needed visit to the lavatories (or to check their email, update their FaceBook and Twitter accounts), Daniel continued his treatise on cultural decline. Mentioning a short list of literary greats, including Faulkner, Steinbeck, Hemingway, et al, he challenged those in attendance to mention even just three contemporary authors who were presently carrying the mantle for—and laudable descendents of—these great literary forebears and legendary authors and who were currently contributing to creating an even greater literary age.

Various authors like Dan Brown, Stephen King and Nicholas Sparks were volunteered by audience members and some jokers shouted out names like Baron Munchausen, Dr. Seuss and Harry Potter. Whether the last three names were said in jest was questionable, as no one was heard laughing in response.

Undeterred, Daniel talked excitedly and passionately about the need for writers and intellectuals to rediscover their passion for the timeless classics and "true" literature. He ranted about the necessity of the re-ignition of "the great quest," (the quest to write the great American novel, that is) and the need, nay, the *urgency* for a renaissance in American literature for which he would lead the way.

Raising his right hand, in a pose reminiscent of a presidential inauguration, Daniel continued: "People before me; fellow citizens of this great nation, to you I make a promise. I vow to be a defender of the hallowed halls of timeless classics, those that make a nation, a culture and a civilization great. With all the innate literary genius and creative wherewithal at my disposal... this is my promise to you. You have put your faith in the right person... I, Daniel Waterstone. Remember that name."

As he paused to take a grand intake of breath, the audience applauded wildly. One got the impression, however, that the rambunctious applause was not so much a validation of his speech and his stated noble quest but more a wild hope that he had concluded and, if not, a ruse to drown out whatever more he might want to say. Many students gave him a standing ovation with mock serious expressions, shouting, "Bravo, Bravo."

Despite her outward show of apathy, a disappointed "Crazy" Mary stood at the rear of the assembled and waited to catch Daniel's eye as he returned to his seat. When he did finally see her and gave her some semblance of acknowledgement, she stuck out her tongue, turned her back, pulled up her weird-looking, homemade, non-traditional gown... and mooned him.

GOING DUTCH

It had been ten years since Daniel's graduation and it's fair to say that the intervening years had not been very kind to him, personally or professionally. Despite some early signs of success, where Daniel acquired a literary agent and had two novels published by a small, yet well regarded, independent publisher, his books did not sell well. His most recent book advance was rapidly approaching complete exhaustion.

Encouraged by his agent to move to a larger metropolis, a shift which she sold to him as a necessary career move (to take meetings and, generally, to be taken seriously by the literary establishment), Daniel moved to Beverly Hills. Soon after that he prudently chose to relocate to West Hollywood and then slowly but surely he continued to down-size and move to less affluent neighborhoods as his funds continued to evaporate.

Upon his final move to a poor and quite noisy neighborhood in the San Fernando Valley, he tempered his self-disappointment with the justification that he was a true artist and like the then unknown and struggling literary expatriates of Paris (Sherwood Anderson, John Dos Passos, F. Scott Fitzgerald, Ernest Hemingway, et al), at the turn of the twentieth century, he too only required a bed, a desk and a typewriter.

His light brown wavy hair made curlier by the heat (and his failure to shower immediately upon waking), Daniel stood over his printer as it printed the remaining few pages of his latest novel, *The Impossible Dream: Part Two*. Bought at the local thrift store, his once-reliable printer was now on its last legs and white streaks were beginning to run down the freshly printed pages. Daniel wiped his sweaty brow and, with excited satisfaction, watched his document print.

Excited about his imminent luncheon appointment with his agent, Suzanne, he was confident that she would not judge him for the poor quality of the manuscript but instead would, once she had read the initial few pages, revel in the prose. In fact, Daniel was one hundred percent sure that the quality of his brilliant writing would obfuscate any short-comings with the print and toner issues in the document. As his new novel was a sequel, he expected it to be a highly desirable property. It answered many questions which were left tantalizingly unanswered in *The Impossible Dream: Part One*.

He didn't want to second guess the publisher's marketing rationale for not having *Part One* out in print yet but he assumed that it was because they were waiting for him to finish *Part Two* so that they could better strategize promotional and marketing opportunities for both books. The publishing and marketing of books was a foreign country to Daniel; one that he didn't know nor truly care to understand but he did appreciate that it was sure to have its intricacies and indeed, for himself and other authors, its necessity.

Like his printer, and most other mechanical and electrical items which he owned, Daniel's fifteen year old car was also on its last legs. As he sat behind the wheel, with ignition key in hand, he made a silent wish that it would start up and without incident transport him to his meeting with Suzanne, on time. Having untold trouble with the vehicle in the past few weeks, he finally had taken it to a mechanic. He had hoped to get a free estimate of its laundry list of issues. Then, he could prioritize repairs and determine what he could afford to have remedied. To his shock, the low ball estimate of the mechanic required a great deal more money than the actual car was worth.

As well as a change of residence (and the repayment of a slew of personal loans, bank and other debts), Daniel needed a new car, or even a new, used one. Back in Illinois, Daniel drove so little that he didn't even remember the model name of his hand-me-down Ford that his father gifted him with. Now living in Los Angeles, where a car was so necessary to one's successful navigation of the sprawling city, Daniel had gotten to know his Toyota Celica more intimately than he had wanted or was even comfortable with.

Thankfully, with the imminent publication of his new novels, he would at last begin to see some financial daylight. He was sure that when the new novels finally hit bookstore shelves, they would be considered revelations in print and reader interest would re-ignite sales of his other two back-list books, *All Alone in an Insane World* and *Heartache*. Financially, things were dire. Yet he was certain that he just had to hang on for a few more weeks.

Daniel turned the vehicle ignition key. The starter motor engaged but the engine didn't turn over. He tried again. And again. On the seventh nail-biting attempt, the car eventually roared into a loud and smoky state of reluctant engagement. The more he drove the vehicle, in its current condition of disrepair, the more he understood the car's dysfunctional state. He knew that if he turned the starter motor repeatedly, for short bursts only, that the car would eventually start up. Once started, he knew that as soon as he took his foot off the gas that the engine would slowly fade and die. Therefore, it was imperative that he keep his foot on the gas.

His challenge, once he got the car moving, was not to let the engine die when he had to slow down or come to a stop. Luckily, the car was a stick shift (which, he was sure, was the reason he got it so cheaply in the first place) and he could depress the clutch while still keeping his foot on the gas pedal, thus preventing the engine from dying. At the very first stop light that Daniel encountered (despite his feet being securely planted on both the clutch and gas pedal), the engine sputtered and died.

Unfortunately, just like life, no amount of planning and understanding is foolproof and with the declining state of the vehicle's overall health, it was getting harder for Daniel to anticipate the car's behavior. His ignition theory was being put to the test and to his chagrin, each and every time he turned the key, his understanding of what worked and didn't work, was found wanting. Despite the number of quick turns of the ignition key, the car would just not start.

In a controlled state of panic, Daniel didn't know what else to do and turned the key so many times without result that the patience of the drivers in the cars stuck behind him began to wear thin and much honking of horns was heard in the otherwise quiet intersection.

Daniel pushed his car to the side of the road and opened the hood more as an act of desperation than as a show of competence. He knew that if he took a good hard look at the wires and coils and tubes and sundry parts of the interior and didn't see something, something which was obviously disconnected or broken or a part that was leaking liquid or protruding smoke, then he had no idea what he was looking at or how to go about fixing.

Sure enough, save for a minor leak in a radiator hose, which he already knew about (and carried a five gallon container of water in the trunk for constant radiator replenishment); he failed to see anything overtly amiss. This was not the first time he had stared cluelessly at the inner sanctum of his increasingly familiar, personal Rubik's cube of an engine. Taking a cloth in one hand he proceeded to tighten and secure everything that looked like it should be tight and secure: wires, tubes and connections of all shapes and sizes.

Having performed the task to his satisfaction, he once again got behind the wheel and turned the key... again and again. After several attempts, the car started. He had no idea why.

Waiting for him at a Beverly Hills adjacent restaurant, Suzanne sipped some imported sparkling water and, on her smart phone, caught up with her emails. Working as a literary agent in a town like Los Angeles, for all these years, Suzanne knew that so much counted on appearances. Meeting clients in restaurants frequented by studio executives, and industry people, in general, was a way of showing that she was busy making deals and that she was in the game. She knew that by being seen she was reinforcing her brand recognition and through her constant presence, advertizing her services. Seeing and being seen meant that she might get a call sooner than a competitor who relied on the telephone directory alone, for new business.

When Daniel finally made it to the underground parking garage, he was shocked to remember that there was no option for motorists to Self Park: everyone had to pull up to the valet stand. As he did so, a Hispanic valet, Carlos, opened his door with a friendly greeting. Daniel, however, did not move from his seat.

"If the engine stops, it won't get started again," Daniel explained, "You need to switch with me."

"Yes," said Carlos, not understanding. He held the door open wider and stood in puzzlement as Daniel remained seated.

"I can't take my foot off of the accelerator," Daniel said more animatedly, realizing that English might not be the valet's first language. "I need you to switch with me to keep the motor running. Understand?"

"Oh. Yes," answered Carlos as he fixed his eyes on Daniel's right foot which remained pressed on the gas pedal, "I put my foot on gas or car die."

"That's right," said Daniel. "I'm sorry but I didn't have time to go to the mechanic."

"Understand," said Carlos, as he gamely extended his foot to replace Daniel's on the gas pedal. In order to do so, he was now practically sitting on Daniel's lap as Daniel tried to slide out from under the valet and scoot over to the passenger side of the car.

"Is your foot on the accelerator?" asked Daniel, masking his embarrassment.

"Yes. Yes, you go," answered Carlos with good sportsmanship cheerfulness.

Leaving Carlos sitting in the driver seat, Daniel grabbed his manuscript and awkwardly opened and then slipped out of the front passenger door. Then he ran around to the other side of the car and, reaching behind the driver's seat, pulled out a large rock which he had kept for this express purpose. He held the rock up to Carlos.

"Okay. When you park it, put this on the gas pedal. If the engine dies, then I'll have to get a…" Daniel didn't finish the sentence because he didn't have any money to call a tow truck and he didn't want to implant the idea into the valet's head that a tow truck was an option.

"Please don't let the engine die. I won't be long."

"Yes, yes, understand."

Daniel watched tensely as Carlos drove the car away. From Carlos' friendly response to the embarrassing episode, Daniel got the impression that Carlos did indeed understand.

"Suzanne, I'm so sorry," Daniel apologized as he

approached Suzanne. Slightly out of breath, he sat and immediately placed his manuscript in her hands. She awkwardly juggled it and then made room for it, placing it on the table.

"Your car broke down," Suzanne said calmly.

"Yes. How did you know?"

"Mechanic's hands," Suzanne said, referring to his somewhat blackened, grease-stained hands. Daniel stared at his hands in embarrassment.

A friendly, yet no nonsense, efficient waiter appeared and smiled as he addressed Daniel. "Can I start you off with a drink? A glass of wine, perhaps?"

Daniel managed to hide his panic and pretended to casually browse the menu. As he looked at the menu options, he was mentally computing what he could order with the nineteen dollars and fifty-two cents cash which he carried in his pocket. As it turned out, what he could pay for, tax and tip included, was not very much. Yet, if he ordered a green salad and a glass of tap water only it would be all too obvious what his pathetic financial situation was.

After a moment's contemplation of etiquette, he decided that it didn't matter. Since the restaurant luncheon was at Suzanne's invitation, he was sure that the accepted, non-written protocol was that the onus to pay was on the inviter and not the invitee. Suzanne was likely to pick up the tab. Then again, he felt that he had to consider the gender factor. If the waiter served the man with the check, which they still tend to do in this day and age of supposed sex equality, then things could get very embarrassing indeed. The waiter hovered, still smiling but looking a tad more impatient. "Do you need a minute?" he asked.

"Yes, please," responded Daniel in a gentle, yet commanding tone. As the waiter shuffled off, Daniel kept his eyes on the menu and mentally wondered how best to ask Suzanne if she was actually paying for this meal.

"Have the steak," Suzanne helpfully suggested. "They're known here for their steaks."

"You're having steak, Suzanne?"

"Can't decide between the tenderloin and the filet mignon. I had the tenderloin here last time and it was exquisite."

"Nice," said Daniel, as he looked at the exorbitant menu prices for both.

"If we both order one of each, we can split them," Suzanne suggested.

"We could do that," Daniel replied unconvincingly. "Don't know if I'm in the mood for steak, though."

The waiter returned and again beamed a smile at Daniel. "Decided on anything to drink?"

"A glass of water would be great. To start with," Daniel said before realizing that there were already two poured glasses of water on the table, complete with ice and a slice of lemon in each.

"Certainly," said the waiter, "domestic or imported?"

"Domestic is fine," said Daniel, wondering what in the heck he had just ordered. At that moment, before his internal panic became external and obvious, Daniel realized that he just had to come out and ask her. So, in as neutral a tone as he could muster, he blurted his query. "How are we doing this, Suzanne? Is this going on your business card as a business expense, is this a business lunch... are you paying?" Daniel asked, all too quickly, his words jumbled together.

Suzanne looked at Daniel for a few beats before answering but it was unclear to Daniel what she may have been thinking.

"Oh, no, honey," Suzanne said with just a slight hint of human feeling, "I assumed we were going to go Dutch."

Daniel wasn't sure if his agent saw his Adam's apple

take an impromptu and uncontrolled leap into the base of his throat but he knew he had to stall with a thoughtful facial expression as it might be a moment before he possessed the ability to speak again.

"Is that a problem?" Suzanne asked.

What Daniel knew was (as did every rapidly, out of control, vibrating cell of his entire body), that this was terrible news on many fronts; it was not merely bad news as far as the present meal was concerned. This was not the, 'the publishers love your novel and can't wait for the next installment' celebratory meal that he had joyfully anticipated.

In his gut, he now knew that this get-together was going to go someplace so ghastly, someplace so terribly, terribly, catastrophically appalling, that he wasn't sure he could take it and hold himself together as a fully functioning human being; which was probably why his agent chose someplace public; someplace where he couldn't shout and scream and throw things and smash whatever was before him into tiny little pieces.

"I can't sell your novel," Suzanne finally said. "I'm sorry."

As Daniel's world imploded upon itself, the waiter returned with another fixed and friendly smile, "How are we doing here? Have you two decided?"

Daniel didn't hear the questions being addressed to him or, if he did, he didn't show it. He looked frozen in place: his body, his face, his unblinking stare... frozen.

"Give us a few more minutes," said Suzanne to the waiter, who once more, and less joyfully this time, shuttled off. Suzanne stared at her client.

"Are you okay, Daniel?"

Daniel did not look at all okay. In fact, if he were a computer, what would be showing would be the blue screen of death, along with the error message, 'a fatal error has occurred and this application cannot continue,' familiar to all PC users, especially those still using operating systems XP and older.

Suzanne watched Daniel with concern and uncertainty as to what to do next. If he truly were a computer, she could simply press control-alt-delete and have him reboot, perhaps restoring him to an acceptable level of functioning. He was not a computer, however, and in any event, as she was not thinking of him as a machine, the thought did not occur to her. Suzanne did, however, wonder if sprinkling him with some drops of water would do the trick. Perhaps a good splash would get him back to the here and now. Before she could consider whether it was best to use imported or domestic, sparkling or tap water, Daniel's eyes blinked.

"Daniel?"

Daniel's facial expression looked as if his brain were indeed rebooting: his eyes flickered and his eyelids fluttered.

"Are you okay?" Suzanne asked.

"You can't sell *The Impossible Dream: Part One*?" Daniel asked, incredulously and hoping that perhaps he had misunderstood her in the first place.

"I'm sorry, Daniel. The market's very soft right now. Maybe down the road."

"It's my best work?" Daniel said with such incomprehension that his statement sounded more like a question.

"It's wonderful, Daniel. It's... a classic."

"Then... what? It needs work? They gave you notes to improve it? What?"

"No, Daniel. They didn't give any notes. They really don't... they feel that they can't take it out, right now."

"They didn't like it?"

"No, they loved it. Everyone thinks it's terrific, your best work yet. It's a minor masterpiece, no question."

"Then why won't they publish it?"

"Because they don't think it will sell, Daniel. They just don't see a market for it. It's not the kind of work that people want to buy, right now."

Suzanne could see that Daniel's brain was trying to understand but couldn't. The wheels were turning and churning but, like changing gears in a car without first engaging the clutch, they couldn't find traction and were screeching like crazy. If Daniel's head was the gearbox, smoke would surely be pouring out his ears. Suzanne remembered prior conversations she had had with him and Daniel hadn't seemed to understand then, either. She wasn't quite sure what his problem was. The situation, as she saw it, was very simple. Was he in denial?

"But you said they would make great feature film script adaptations... that I was going to sell a ton of books... that you believed in me," Daniel said mournfully.

"I did... I do believe in you," Suzanne replied in a measured tone of voice, "I thought your work would sell and that we could do some movie deals, too. The marketplace hasn't born that out."

"But maybe—"

"Daniel, we discussed this before with your other novels," Suzanne spoke slowly and methodically. "Nobody is buying what you write. No one is buying your books. I don't know how else to say it. Your work has no commercial appeal. It's unfortunate."

Daniel did remember having this conversation before, concerning his two books in print which were languishing at the bottom of the sales rankings. "That's because they're not being promoted. If my books get no promotion, of course they won't sell."

Suzanne was still hungry and was now beginning to wonder if she was going to get to eat lunch at all. She hadn't had breakfast and was tired already of the conversation but she would humor him a little longer, if they could actually order and get some food. Raising her hand to flag down the passing waiter, she gestured to Daniel, 'one moment.'

"Ready to order?" asked the waiter, his relief showing.

"Do me a favor, honey," Suzanne said to the waiter, handing him back the menus. "We're in a bit of a hurry. Bring us out a couple of the house burgers, medium rare, with a side of fries. Thanks a bunch." Happy to finally get a food order, the waiter didn't hesitate with any further food or drink questions and headed straight for the kitchen.

"My treat," Suzanne quickly said to Daniel. "Don't worry about it."

"*The Literary Monitor* called *All Alone in an Insane World* an instant classic! *Heartache* was a book of the month pick in the *Times*. Even *The Kranky Review* raved about *Heartache*, calling it 'an unqualified, critical success.' Remember?" said Daniel, his head still trying to make sense of the present reality.

"Absolutely, no question," countered Suzanne, hoping the burgers would get served right away, "but, unfortunately, nobody reads book reviews anymore. Maybe a handful of snobs and professors on the East coast but the buying public?" Suzanne made a gesture, 'forget about it.' She then paused before dropping the next bombshell. "The publishers would also like to have their advance returned."

"What?"

"The advance they gave you to write the new book. They want it back."

"But... I wrote the book. Here it is. I'm delivering it on time."

"It's not a time issue, Daniel. It's in the contract somewhere: if either or both parties decide not to proceed within the allotted time frame... something like that. Don't worry. I'll talk to them about it."

"Don't worry, they don't want the advance back or don't worry, you'll talk to them about them wanting the advance back?"

"I need someone in legal to look at that particular clause. Having to return an advance is pretty rare," Suzanne said, returning his manuscript to him.

Daniel took the manuscript and stared at it, in shock that, yes, he was, in fact, having to take the manuscript back home with him. Not only that, there was a possibility of having to return money which he no longer had and had no way in the world of coming up with. The ramifications of it all were mind-boggling to him.

"Are you working on anything else, right now?" Suzanne asked, as she asked of all her clients when what was being proffered was unsuitable to her needs. Daniel didn't break his stare at the manuscript now in his own hands and it seemed to Suzanne that he might be retreating back into brain freeze mode. "Maybe if I took a look?" she said, hoping to get his attention.

"You don't understand," said Daniel, not raising his eyes, "I don't have anything else. This was it. This *is* it." Daniel carefully held the manuscript like it was a delicate new born baby and slowly brought it to his chest, cradling it. "I poured my soul into these pages... agonized over every single word, every phrase, every description... every vowel. You have no idea," he said, deeply and enigmatically. "You have no idea."

"You're a wonderful writer, Daniel. I mean it," Suzanne said with one eye on the kitchen door. Where were those hamburgers?

As if every sinew and muscle in Daniel's body were losing the fight to stay taut and keep his body erect and upright, the muscles in Daniel's torso became loose and limp. Unable or unwilling to fight the forces of gravity anymore, Daniel's body began slowly sinking down into his chair. "I poured my soul into these pages," he said.

"I was touched. I was really very touched." Suzanne picked up her phone.

"I thought that this was the one. I really did," said Daniel then he slipped further down into his chair. "I thought I had it licked with this one."

"You write such beautiful characters," Suzanne said, checking her phone for emails.

"My life is meaningless. I'm sinking into a vast bottomless pit and I can't do anything about it," Daniel said as he slid down in his chair to the floor below.

"There are no words to describe it, Daniel. Rejection sucks. Daniel?"

Daniel had vanished beneath the table. Wary of his melodramatic leanings in the past, Suzanne, was not prepared for this eventuality: an author's total meltdown. She pulled up the tablecloth and looked below to see what she was dealing with. Daniel sat on the floor beneath the table, rocking to and fro, cradling the script to his chest. "My baby, oh, my baby..." he repeated to himself.

"Daniel. Are you okay?"

"Nobody wants my baby. I don't understand. Nobody wants my baby."

"I have an idea," Suzanne said, thinking fast, cognizant that shortly their table would become a laughingstock to the other diners. "Give me the manuscript and I'll make some more calls. The novel is so... brilliant, someone out there must see its value and want to give it a good home. What do you say?"

Daniel stopped his rocking and with a hopeful expression turned to look at Suzanne.

"Let me try find it a good home," Suzanne said gently, her arm extended.

"And a check," said Daniel. "Don't forget the check."

"Of course," said Suzanne, helping him to his feet.

§

Down below, in the underground parking garage, as Daniel waited for his car to be brought round, he realized that he was still holding his manuscript. He turned in panic, looking to see Suzanne, who, just a moment ago, had been walking right behind him.

Carlos drove up in Daniel's car and smiling to Daniel, he proudly held up the rock. "I keep the engine going, see?"

"Yes. Thank you," Daniel said, thankful but woefully embarrassed at the same time. How did it come to this, he wondered. Suzanne exited the elevators and gave her ticket to a waiting valet.

"Suzanne!" Daniel yelled to her, holding aloft the script. "You forgot the manuscript."

Suzanne acted like she didn't want to talk anymore. "No, Daniel. I didn't forget it."

"I thought you said you were going to find it a good home?" Daniel asked, puzzled.

"You were embarrassing me, Daniel. I lied. I couldn't allow you to continue to jeopardize my reputation as an agent with your behavior... so I said what I needed to say to prevent that."

Daniel's car backfired and the engine began to sputter, threatening to die. "Pump the gas. Pump the gas!" Daniel admonished Carlos. Carlos pumped the gas: the car roared back to life. Daniel gestured "one minute" to Carlos and approached Suzanne.

"But I need your help, Suzanne," Daniel pleaded.

Suzanne put a pair of obviously expensive, beautiful sunglasses on and pulled out a silk, designer scarf. "Daniel, I'm sorry. I know things are tight, right now, but I make it a rule never to—"

"I'm not looking for money," Daniel interrupted. "I need some creative advice."

"I'm running late, Daniel," Suzanne said and folded the beautiful scarf into a triangle and tied it over her head. Her ensemble was now complete and ever-so chic.

"If nobody wants to sell the novels I write... What am I supposed to do? Wait for the market to cycle around and become interested... down the road? Do I keep writing what I'm writing?" Daniel queried, his voice trembling with raw panic. He rubbed his fingers on his forehead and tried to release the tension that was building there.

Suzanne's late model convertible was brought around by the valet and she wasted no time getting into it. "Call me at the office, okay?" It was obvious from her tone that she did not really wish for Daniel to give her a call.

"Do I write what the market wants? Do I write something... that will sell? What is the market buying these days?" he asked, desperation making him look unattractive and pathetic.

"You're a fine writer, Daniel. Write what you know. Write what's in your heart." With a wave, Suzanne drove off.

"Nobody cares to read what's written in my heart," Daniel said, and it came out a soft growl, as his throat was tight with emotion. He watched her drive away.

With his head held low, Daniel trudged to his car and, taking into consideration his serious financial predicament, gave Carlos an astronomical tip. He then carefully exchanged places with Carlos, being certain that someone's foot was depressing the gas pedal the entire time, so that the engine wouldn't die.

MIND MELD WITH ME

On his return home, Daniel drove with extreme apprehension as he approached a busy intersection where stop and go traffic was the norm. Increasingly common, as of late, the car began to overheat. The temperature gauge crawled steadily up towards the red.

A little tip Daniel had picked up on the internet was to turn the car heater on full blast, which he now did. Although the trick helped prevent the engine temperature from rising too rapidly, allied with the ninety-plus degree temperature of sunny Los Angeles, the extra heat blasting from the dashboard vents had the effect of rising Daniel's own temperature to an intolerable, verging on sadistic, level. Rolling down all the car windows was poor consolation and did little to improve his personal over-heated condition. He sweltered, and the running of the heater at full blast sadly put additional strain on the pitiable battery which was being insufficiently charged by a sub-par alternator.

Despite all his best efforts, just as he came to his third stop in the crawling traffic, the engine died. Frantically turning the ignition key again and again, Daniel prayed with mental savagery that the engine would turn over and get him home safely. Mentally, he made a pact with the car. He promised the vehicle that, if it did start, he would not take it out again until he had the money to get it fixed—if it would only start right now. He mentally made an oath, to the car, that he would never mistreat it in such a fashion, ever again. He gave the car his solemn word.

The car, however, remained unresponsive to his pleas. Perhaps the vehicle is just too far gone, Daniel reasoned.

Behind him, drivers honked and yelled, some suggesting that he get that "piece of shit car off of the fucking road."

Daniel kept turning the key until the battery became so weak that it lost the required charge to turn over the engine. He had no choice but to push his car to the side of the road and plan his strategy from there. With one hand on the steering wheel, one hand holding open the door, Daniel leaned his shoulder against the door frame and heaved. With great effort, he slowly pushed the vehicle, almost the length of the entire long block, until he found a spot away from red zones and parking meters. The parking sign said that he could park there legally, for two hours.

Fortunately for him, he determined, he did not need two hours to decide on a course of action. In truth, he had very little choice. Even if he could afford to get the automobile towed to a mechanic, he did not have the funds required to get the vehicle fixed. If he got the car towed to a street near his apartment, he'd still be bound by parking restrictions and would have to move it or suffer a series of parking tickets which required immediate payment under threat of heftier fines and ultimately imprisonment. The auto had to go.

Daniel wasn't certain how to successfully abandon a car, as it was his very first time. Even though it sounded like a book title that he might have came across on the web someplace, he hadn't read the book in question. In his poor and weak frame of mind, he had to make quick decisions. He felt that, even if it were the best of times, he was poorly equipped to make these kinds of choices. Yet he must.

Luckily, the car possessed little in the way of identifiable items which could be traced to him directly. Obviously, he would take his manuscript and everything in the glove compartment that had his name and address on it. He figured that he would also need to remove the license plates and remove the Vehicle Identification Numbers wherever he could find them.

Having performed to satisfaction all of those tasks which he'd determined were required, Daniel stood back from the car and mentally thanked it for all its hard years of service. He had grown fond of his little Celica over the years and, as unusual as it may seem, he had come to believe that the car had a personality all of its own.

He had learned from its responsiveness, in terms of how he drove it, what the car liked and didn't like. It didn't like driving in low gear, for instance. It detested stop and go traffic, where it had a tendency to express its displeasure by overheating and, if he persisted in driving it under those conditions, the engine would start to sputter. It didn't like sharp turns at high speed; the tires would scream their disapproval. It did like cruising in fifth gear and the open road in general, especially on freeways away from the city and up the coast near the ocean. It seemed to really like the open road, which unfortunately, Daniel hadn't being seeing much of in quite some time.

Daniel chucked the license plates in a nearby trash can and began his walk home in earnest. He contemplated taking a bus but he had no way of knowing which one to take. He was afraid of taking a bus that looked like it was going in the right direction but might instead take one unfamiliar turn too many and leave him in an unknown area, even further away than from where he started. He made a mental note to study bus routes online as this would now be his new mode of local transportation.

As he crossed a busy intersection, his attention was aroused by a line of people who were lining up in the mid-day sun holding a book in their hands. He was familiar with bookish-looking crowds that lined up for book-signing events, and this certainly looked like one, but who would be signing books in Studio City—in the Valley, no less—on a Thursday afternoon? The line snaked around the corner so he couldn't see their eventual destination: is there even a book store in Studio City, he wondered. Standing there in the hot early afternoon sun, he felt an intense desire, almost a compulsion, to know what book those people were holding and where they were going. He decided to go and investigate.

Walking past the line of eager bibliophiles, Daniel did indeed discover that the line of sweating bodies - the ugly and the beautiful of Los Angeles - terminated inside a large bookstore. An ostentatious life-sized cut-out of the author was prominently displayed in the entrance to the books store, along with a sandwich board that read: *Take Control of Your Life!* Randy Guswhite Book Signing Today. The book in question, *Take Control of Your Life!* took up the entire front window display. Not knowing this obviously popular, best-selling author and curious beyond measure, Daniel entered the store.

The author in question, who, at first glance, looked like a normal guy, sat at a table busily signing copies of his book. Keeping one eye on the book-signing spectacle, Daniel casually strolled to the literature section to search for his own books. Because sales were flat, he wondered if the publisher was actually getting them into bookstores, at all. He had to look long and hard before finding a single copy of each of his titles, which were misplaced on the bottom shelf. He placed them face-up on the top shelf in the most prominent position that he could find.

Daniel watched as the line of book buyers eagerly fixed their eyes on the author as they approached. They were clearly awestruck. There was a tension in the air which was almost sexual. Daniel could see that even bookstore browsers, who probably hadn't known about the signing, were snatching up the few remaining copies of the book from a large table display.

What was it about this author and his book that was creating such enthusiasm among its readers, Daniel wondered. A nerdy-looking couple stood beside Daniel, smiles on their faces, comparing the autographs which they had each received from the author.

"Have you read this guy?" Daniel casually asked them.

"I was nobody before I discovered Randy," the nerdy woman replied.

"Who are you now?" Daniel asked, without a hint of sarcasm.

"I'm a more fully developed person," the woman answered, "You should read this book. It will change your life." Daniel glanced at the blurb of the proffered book: *Unlock the untapped potential of your brain! Get anything you want, simply by thinking it into existence! Contains powerful mind over matter exercises to help you actualize your latent thought energy...*

"We used to live in a fog but Randy has shown us how to live life to our full potential," the young man raved.

"Do yourself a favor and read this book," the young woman said, and gestured toward the dwindling copies on the display table. Then she took her autographed copy and walked off with her equally-enamored boyfriend. Daniel didn't know what to make of it all: get anything you want by thinking into existence? Seriously?

"Ever seen such crap?" a male voice said. Daniel turned to see a clean-cut, bespectacled short man in a business suit. "It's a sad state of affairs when books like this take up the whole front of the store. Decent books get no shelf space," the man continued. Daniel noticed a box of new books at the man's feet.

"Tell me about it," Daniel agreed.

"You're a writer?"

"Yeah. You?"

"Let me give you a tip," the strange little man said, adopting a conspiratorial tone, "Self publish, self promote. In these end times, it's the only way to go."

"End times?" asked Daniel. The man gave Daniel a copy of one of his books, "*The End Times: What You Need to Know about the Alien Plot to End All Life.*"

"Catchy title," said Daniel, handing the book back.

"People need to know what's *really* going on," the man said and squinted his eyes, for no apparent reason. Then he returned the book to his box and walked to the counter. Daniel stared after him and heard the man ask to speak to the manager.

Daniel watched as reader after reader approached best-selling author Randy Guswhite, purchased book in hand, extended for an autograph. Daniel couldn't help but feel envious. As a young boy growing up, this was exactly the future he had imagined for himself. In fact, this very scenario had been an image in his head since, well, forever: him, Daniel, a best-selling author signing autographs for his adoring public.

What is wrong with the world, Daniel wondered. He knew the worth of his writing; it was brilliant or at the very least, above average. Yet here was the gullible - and evidently misguided - public lining up for an audience with a weird snake-oil salesman who was either an out and out fraud or, if he really believed in the idiocy that he was writing, a certifiable crazy person.

Daniel sidled closer to get a better look at the fraudster and now noticed that even the man's anatomy was oddly distorted. He had unusually large hands, yet a rather small head and massive feet. His legs were long, yet his torso was short and stocky. He wore a beard, probably to shield a weak jaw, yet his nose was on the large size. He did possess piercing blue eyes. Daniel could appreciate the author's effect on the more gullible members of the public. There was something quite charismatic about his presence. Then again, apparently there was something charismatic about Machiavelli, Svengali and Charles Manson, to name but three notorious crazy people of history, both real and fictionalized.

As Daniel got closer, he heard what this strange man was saying to his devoted followers. "You gave me a new reason to believe in myself and strive to reach my peak," a middle-aged woman said to him as she held out her book.

"What is your name?" the author asked.

"Ursula. Ursula Mesher."

As Randy Guswhite stood up, Daniel had to stand back a little: he was not expecting the guy to be so tall. He towered over little Ursula Mesher but, for some reason, she was not afraid and kept smiling. The giant author extended his long, giant arm and placed his monster-like hand on Ursula's head. He then closed his eyes, as if in deep concentration. The adoring fans huddled in tight groups and watched fixedly at their master at work.

"Your weakness is fear," the giant bellowed from above. Daniel sniggered uncontrollably and turned to see who else was amused. He reined in his smile when he noticed a fan glaring at him and realized that he was the sole philistine. His blasphemous snort did not go unnoticed by the giant.

"Every decision we take in life is grounded in either love or in fear," the tall man said. "You must be brave, Ursula. You must work on conquering those fears."

"I will. I will," Ursula quickly resolved.

The author looked slowly and deliberately at his reverential audience, as if scanning each face, much in the way that a king would scan the faces of his court, looking for facial expressions of either adoration or disdain. "There is someone here who is afraid to live," he said, ominously. Daniel could see that the crowd was holding their collective breath, each individual hoping that, for the love of God, it wasn't them.

"Lack of belief is a fear of life, itself. You who cannot believe, have only death to look forward to," the author said in a sing-song-like chant. A couple of fans moaned in appreciation. Daniel managed to suppress a snort of derision yet unconsciously shook his head in abject disbelief. Not only was he amazed at the over-the-top showmanship of the fraudster but he was also entirely fascinated by the obviously gullible nature of his self-appointed devotees.

"You!" Randy bellowed as he swung his long arm and turned his giant frame to point directly at Daniel. "You, sir, are engulfed by fear!"

"What, now?" Daniel heard himself say but he wasn't sure if he actually said it out loud.

"Every single, solitary cell in your body is conquered by fear!"

Daniel suddenly felt himself regressing to a small boy that had done something wrong; as the crowd retreated from his space and isolated him. Daniel saw in their eyes a reaction of disgust and withdrawal. They looked at him as if he had leprosy.

"If you could see the aura emanating from your body, sir, you would see how diseased and convoluted you are inside," the large man continued, as he walked closer towards Daniel.

As skeptical and as reasoned as Daniel believed himself to be, he could not prevent the fear inside of him from rearing up. It caught him in the throat and caused his knees to become inordinately weak. If the giant wore a dark robe, he could easily have passed as an evil wizard in any Hollywood B movie of the forties and fifties.

"What is your name?" the wizard inquired.

"I, ur, um…" Daniel's vocal chords were too tight to speak.

Without asking permission, Randy placed one of his mighty hands on top of Daniel's head. Daniel remained even more frozen as the big man closed his eyes and tightly concentrated. The crowd watched, in rapt silence, as Randy made weird, disconcerting facial expressions, as if he had tasted something horrible.

"There's so much fear, I can't… I can't…" Breaking away, Randy's eyes opened wide as if from a bad dream. "I can't read anything!" he exclaimed incredulously. The crowd gasped.

"Are you a practitioner?" he asked an equally dumbfounded Daniel.

"A what?" asked Daniel as he gladly found his voice and his reason returning. "I'm a writer, as a matter of fact"

"You write books similar to mine?"

"No," replied Daniel. "I write literature. You obviously write comedies."

The crowd reacted like they never heard such blasphemy and began gossiping menacingly amongst themselves. If it had been the Middle Ages, Daniel was sure he would be headed for a stoning. Randy quickly raised both his hands, his palms facing Daniel. "Mind meld with me," he said in all earnestness.

"What?"

"Press your finger tips against mine. Thought transference. It works."

Daniel was not a science fiction aficionado but he knew that what this strange man was requesting was something that he had seen on a TV show somewhere, at some time, quite possibly an episode of Star Trek or The Twilight Zone.

"Your fear paralyzes you?" the big man taunted.

Daniel looked around at all the expectant faces. He had never been to a live hypnotist show but he imagined that everyone in attendance had and were quite possibly the very people who would raise their hands when the showman asked for volunteers.

Fine, he thought to himself, let them have their show. Let them be witness to a master hypnotist failing miserably when he finally takes on a subject who, under no circumstances, will allow himself to be tricked, duped or deceived by a grand rascal.

Daniel raised his finger tips and touched them against those of the giant's. Looking him straight in the eyes, Daniel said to himself: Superman... meet Kryptonite.

"Now, place your forehead against mine," said Superman. Daniel looked at him with the expression, 'You've got to be kidding me.'

"Afraid I'll extract the contents of your skeptical mind?" the giant intoned drily.

"I'm more concerned that I might extract the scary content of yours. If there is anything in there at all, that is," said Daniel who felt himself getting bolder by the second. Let's give these fools a real kick in the butt, he said to himself as he watched their terrified-looking expressions.

"Think of nothing," Randy advised. "Let your mind go blank."

Daniel mentally corrected him, the proper phrase being, "Don't think of anything." Then he decided, what the heck, when in Rome... he would play along and think of nothing, or at least, nothing of consequence. He wasn't afraid of being hypnotized by the wizard. He would not unknowingly be made of fool of, take down his pants, or upon being given a hypnotic suggestion, run amongst the crowd, clucking like a chicken.

It was the idiocy of the moment; their touching fingertips, almost holding hands, and placing his forehead against the forehead of a complete stranger in a rundown bookstore in the San Fernando Valley which caused him to wonder: just exactly how did I get here? That thought led him to the subsequent thought: I wonder where my life is headed. How did I get so off track with my life?

What happened to all that potential he was blessed with as a youth? He wasn't old, or over the hill, by any stretch of the imagination but surely at this stage of his life he should have made strides, become a man of influence, stature, a distinguished man-of-letters with a devoted following, eagerly anticipating his next major work.

He should already be travelling in literary circles (perhaps being bestowed honorary doctorates) and invited to speak at major literary events. He should by now have been given the opportunity, by invitation, to teach as a visiting professor, to any of the big three colleges, with an ancillary stipend to tide him over while he completed his next major opus. Yes, that would be a step in the right direction.

What has happened to this once great country, he wondered, when fools like this are being feted and those with true talent are not even recognized, much less respected and lauded? By their very nature, idiots do not have the intellectual capacity to identify genius. All that idiots are mentally equipped to recognize are other idiots.

"I... nothing's coming," said the leader of the idiots, his facial contortions expressing either real or fake difficulty, Daniel could not tell. "You're not in a relaxed state of mind," he admonished a bemused Daniel. What is this guy's act, wondered Daniel. He's passing himself off as some kind of mind reader? Randy broke from the mind meld, stood back from Daniel, and looked at him with extreme confusion. "I can't read anything," he said, acting as if this were a first for him. "There's so much fear inside you... it must have taken you over."

"Or perhaps you're not used to coming face to face with someone who possesses a thinking brain; a brain that's not merely... vacuous," Daniel said as he looked at the assembled faces of indeterminate expressions.

"What's wrong with you people?" Daniel said to the hushed gathering. "What has become of independent thought? Don't you people question, or even reason, anymore? You are endowed with free and self-governing thought and yet you have given up your thought processes to rely on others to tell you what is real and to inform you of what is of value? That's no "mind meld" but instead... mental slavery." Looking somewhat chastened, some of those gathered, lowered their eyes.

"Think about it," Daniel continued. "You have willingly volunteered your brains, your thought processes... your consciousness... your will and even your identity, to be programmed and controlled by false prophets such as he. My, my..." said Daniel, shaking his head, the gravity of the state of the world bearing heavy on his very soul and psyche. The crowd murmured amongst themselves, the balance of power seeming to shift.

"Denial, my friend!" Randy bellowed loudly, perhaps fearing that he was losing the crowd. "Fear and denial. Seek help. Seek help before it strangles you to death!"

Daniel took one long and last sorry look at the assembled acolytes and then locked eyes with the once great and mighty, but now visibly shaken, defeated author.

"Bite me," Daniel said and then he turned and left.

WHAT THE MARKET WANTS

Curious to know with whom he had been recently mind-melding, Daniel decided to stop by his local library and pick up a copy of the author's book. As he walked the long stretch back to his own neighborhood, he wondered at just how out of touch he was with the reading habits of the average person and indeed, with modern culture, in general.

Save for the occasional documentary on the local PBS channels, he didn't watch TV. He had no idea what the top ten TV shows were. He didn't listen to modern music but was content to listen to his favorite composers, varying his choice dependent upon his mood: Mozart, Haydn or perhaps Sibelius when he was feeling cheerful; Mahler, Bach, Shostakovich or quite likely Rachmaninoff when he was feeling sad. As far back as he could remember he had always harbored a deep-seated feeling - almost a certainty - that he was born into the wrong age.

When he finally reached the library, he walked directly to the Librarian's desk. He smiled when he saw that his good friend Mavis was on duty. Like himself, Mavis was old school. She had a deep and abiding love for the classics, over which, like two peas in a pod, they bonded. It made no difference that Mavis was in her eighties; her mind was sharp and her sensibilities matched those of Daniel's to a tee.

"Daniel," Mavis greeted him with a warm smile. "Haven't seen you in quite some time. You must have finished your book."

"I have, Mavis, thank you. How have you been?"

"Just dandy, Daniel. Just dandy. What can I get for you today?"

"Two things, Mavis. I need a copy of a book by an author called Randy Guswhite…"

"Oh, dear," Mavis instinctively said and it appeared to Daniel that her bosoms may have heaved, ever-so-slightly, from concern.

"I know," Daniel said, defensively. "It's purely for research, I assure you."

"What's the second thing that you need?" Mavis said judiciously.

"The second thing I need is to buy you a cup of coffee. What time is your break?"

"My break is whenever I say it is," Mavis said and winked at Daniel with a mischievous grin. "However, the book in question, whose title I won't even deign to mention, is a best-seller, which defies all reason. There is a waiting list, almost a hundred names long."

"Surely you jest," said Daniel, shocked out of his mind.

"It's unreadable and yet it is flying off of the shelves. However, it's not the first nor, I'm sure, the last time that I will be flummoxed by popular reading habits."

"Which is exactly why I need to talk to you. I know that if anybody can understand my predicament, it will be you."

"What predicament is that, sweetie?" Mavis smiled kindly. She genuinely cared about Daniel, and his unnamed dilemma, and it made him feel safe somehow.

"I'll explain over coffee. Our usual place in say… fifteen minutes?"

"I'll be there."

Daniel and Mavis' usual place was a funky little coffee shop within walking distance of the library. It attracted a more bohemian crowd than the chain store down the block. It was mostly populated by single people working on laptops or reading books. Knowing exactly what Mavis liked, Daniel had already ordered beverages for them both before Mavis actually arrived.

"A copy of the book was just returned," she said to Daniel as she handed him Randy Guswhite's book, *Take Control of your Life!* "If anybody asks, you took it from the sorting shelves." Then she dazzled him with a smile. Daniel smiled back.

"You're a darling," he said. "Thanks for that." She nodded in response.

"So, what's all this about? This strange book request and your "predicament?""

"They're not going to publish *The Impossible Dream: Part One* and, in fact, it sounds like they're pulling all of my books and are threatening to ask for the return of their advance," said Daniel, sounding reasoned and calm and totally out of touch with his hysterical inner panic.

"Oh, dear," was all Mavis could manage to say, considering the enormity of Daniel's distressing news.

"It's not like I could easily get a job or something. All I've done for the past ten years is write literary novels... a very slim resume, you must agree."

"Do you want to get a job?"

"Of course not. I'm a writer. I want to write."

"Well, then."

"If nobody is buying books that I write, then perhaps I need to be writing books that people will want to buy. Correct?"

"I could see the sense to that, yes."

"So. What are people reading these days?"

"Oh, dear," said Mavis with a heavy heart.

"What?" asked Daniel, now a little concerned.

"I'm not sure you want to know the answer to your questions."

"I don't see where I have any other choice. Do you? I certainly don't want to starve to death, which at this point is a definite possibility."

"Oh, dear," said Mavis again.

"Please stop saying that, Mavis. I know I'm foraging for scraps here but you have to help me out and stay strong for me," Daniel admonished, "after all, I'm the one facing disaster."

"Well, one look at the best-seller list should tell you anything you want to know, Daniel. People don't read to enlighten themselves or seek to gain some valuable insight into their own… psychology. People are not looking for books that help shine a light on or question the human condition. People read to escape."

"Escape, what?" Daniel asked, his voice colored by his incredulity.

"Escape their lives, of course. Look around you, Daniel. People are miserable and are leading lives filled with a mix of boredom and pain. Books help them to escape all that."

Daniel looked around the coffee shop. Almost every person present had earphone wires hanging from their ears. Some were reading on an electronic device while listening to music; some were watching videos or surfing the web. Despite the fact that they all seemed preoccupied, they nonetheless did appear like they were masking some secret, inner pain.

"I see," said Daniel, thoughtfully. "*Most men lead lives of quiet desperation and go to the grave with the song still in them,*" he said, quoting Thoreau.

"Thoreau was correct then and even more so now. Let me tell you something, Daniel," said Mavis, leaning closer to him. "The only reason people come to my library is so that they can borrow the best sellers, use the internet and check out the latest DVDs. If all we had was a literature section, then I'd be out of a job, along with the rest of the staff."

"Okay, now I'm really depressed," said Daniel and his voice was as low as his heart.

"You can't argue with what is Daniel, and wishing it were something different is only going to make matters worse, for you in particular. If you don't move with the times, you get left behind and you become irrelevant. We must reinvent ourselves in every moment, that's my motto." Daniel stared at his dear elderly friend and took time to admire not just her wisdom but her seemingly indefatigable love of life, itself.

"I appreciate your honesty, Mavis, I really do. This may be depressing news but you're helping me a great deal. Just one more thing. What genres *are* the best sellers?"

"There are really only three genres that everyone wants to read and then everything else is a subset or a combination, thereof," the beautiful and wise old crone stated simply.

"Which is?" Daniel asked, his voice quavering with true interest.

"The big trinity of publishing: mystery, thrillers and romance. If you can combine all three, then it's a winner's trifecta and you'll be rich beyond your dreams."

"I see. But what about all those vampire and zombie books or the young adult ones... the ones about people with superhuman or paranormal abilities... aren't those hot genres?"

"Romance, mystery, thriller with zombies or goblins or elves or super heroes... just different ingredients in the same stew. Now, I have to get back to my desk. Someone might get into a tizzy trying to find the latest Tom Clancy." Mavis finished her drink and stood.

"You've been a big help, Mavis and I especially thank you for the book."

"If nothing else, it should give you a good laugh," Mavis said as she stood to leave. "Don't be a stranger." Mavis smiled down at him and it was as if the sun were shining on Daniel. They were genuinely fond of each other. She was truly a bright spot in his otherwise, dreary life.

"I won't. You may be seeing much more of me now, while I research my next book," Daniel said, standing up.

"Lovely. Do you even know what the topic of your next book will be?"

"I haven't a clue," said Daniel, walking Mavis to the door. "Where does this book fit in with your best-seller theory? I don't even know what genre this is."

"The success of that book and others like it just goes to prove my point. People are lost and some of them are looking for answers. The fact that this book is a best seller merely goes to show how severe the problems of humanity really are. As long as the world, and the people in it, feels hopeless and lost, there will always be opportunistic imposters trying to cash in on the misery of others. You should stop around at my place sometime for a more prolonged visit but I really must be getting back."

Deep in thought, Daniel held the door open for Mavis to leave. "Take care of yourself, Mavis. You're a good friend."

"I'm your only friend, Daniel. I keep telling you to get out more." He kissed her on the cheek and waved to her as she left.

Daniel returned to his seat to finish his coffee. He looked over the book that Mavis had brought to him, scanning the table of contents and flicking through some random chapters. The subject category on the back said it was "Self Help/Personal Transformation," which meant absolutely nothing to him. It seemed to be peppered throughout with meaningless statements which were given prominence in bold lettering, each of them invariably being punctuated with an exclamation mark: Be Bold! Decide That You Can Do It! There is Nothing That You Cannot Achieve! Use the Laws of Attraction and Make It Count! Believe in Yourself!

Along with inspirational quotes by famous authors, some of them quite nice, he had to admit (but also a sure sign of an author with little original to say who was padding his book with the genius of others), there were also a series of exercises. The exercises were supposedly designed to reprogram, "redesign" and expand the reader's brain for greater use and function.

Aside from being decidedly questionable in their merits, some of the exercises were just downright nuts. Driving a different route home from work and writing with the opposite hand for a change, sounded pretty harmless but, "Do something that you wouldn't normally do!" did not seem like sound advice to give to someone with questionable morals or someone who was already on the verge of lunacy.

Exercises like walking backwards around the house, doing several tasks at once (the book actually recommended walking and chewing gum at the same time), listening to music in the darkness and closing one's eyes while taking a shower were purported to "activate latent regions of the brain and awake quiescent neurons from their slumber." Smelling things you wouldn't ordinarily sniff was said to awaken and expand olfactory neurons and give the reader's life a richer experience. You could not make this stuff up, Daniel thought to himself. The material was comical and ever-so-ripe for parody. And yet, the book was a best seller. The world makes little sense, he thought, as he closely regarded the book in his hand.

That night, back at his studio apartment, Daniel did sit

in the dark, while he pondered deeply. He wasn't deliberately trying to expand his brain; his power had been cut off due to a misunderstanding with the electric company, which involved one-too-many late payments. He determined that he needed to write something fast. It would have to be a book that would sell well enough to ease his immediate financial stress and tide him over while he wrote *The Impossible Dream: Part Three*, which would finally conclude the series.

He gave himself emotional succor, by reminding himself that it was no disgrace to be poor. Many great writers had suffered even greater poverty than he was experiencing, yet managed to survive and, eventually, to thrive. Charles Dickens experienced horrendous poverty and wrote serials for the monthly letterpress - the magazines of the day - in order to put food on the table. James Joyce owed money to half the denizens of Paris while working on his masterpieces, which were at the time considered the unpublishable scribblings and ravings of a demented person.

Daniel sat in the increasing darkness and mused further. Eric Blair had lived in the slums of the two major European cities of the day and later wrote of his experiences in the book, *Down and out in Paris and London* which he wrote under the pen name of George Orwell. His literary classic, a satire of what he described as, "the moral and emotional shallowness of our time," *Animal Farm* was soundly rejected by publishers on both sides of the Atlantic. Alfred Knopf reportedly rejected it by saying that it was "impossible to sell animal stories in the U.S.A."

Mystery, thriller and romance, Daniel said to himself, mulling over the possibilities.

Each genre had its specific conventions, story structure and reader expectations. He wasn't sure that he was confident or even interested enough to pursue such genre writing. Even if he did know where to start, in writing a mystery or a thriller, he knew that what he might come up with would be like none other on the market. It might not end up resembling any of the thrillers or mysteries that readers of such genres would recognize or desire and buy. As for romance? He had never had one. He reasoned that that tiny detail might put him at a certain disadvantage in writing a romance novel.

Besides, he didn't want to pimp out his genuine talents and become a hack, just to sell books and become "popular." So, just like Samuel Clemens (Mark Twain), Charles Dodgson (Lewis Carroll), Currer Bell (Charlotte Bronte) and many others before him, he would write under a pseudonym. But write what, he wondered to himself.

Fumbling toward his bed, in the darkness, he lay his head down and thought about his earlier conversation with Mavis, the authors he greatly admired and the Guswhite book. A notion began to form in his mind. He wasn't quite sure what the idea was but he was aware that, just like all of his other creative musings in the past, his subconscious mind was working on a solution. He knew that, based upon past experience, the solution would pop into his conscious mind when it was well and truly formulated. All he had to do was rest, do something else, totally unrelated, and trust that the answer would come. Surrendering to his exhausted state, he closed his eyes and allowed his subconscious mind the temporary ownership of his brain and sundry mental faculties.

After a fitful night's sleep, filled with appalling dreams which he cared not to remember, Daniel awoke. He was only mildly surprised to see that it was almost noon. Having the least bit of stress in his life had a tendency to throw off his sleeping patterns and prevent his body and mind from achieving that basic health requirement of all humans: deep, restorative sleep.

With his head still in a brain fog, he staggered to the bathroom to release the contents of his bladder. It was whilst he was mindlessly watching his bodily fluids enter the toilet bowl that the solution - the topic of his next book - came popping up into his thoughtless head. Of course! he exclaimed to himself. The minor eureka moment cheered him up and woke his brain cells from their lethargic slumber. That's it! he almost shouted. I'll start it right away, he decided.

HOW NOT TO WRITE A BEST-SELLER

With joyful excitement, which he hadn't experienced in quite a long while, Daniel placed a stack of books on the desk before a mystified Mavis.

"What are all these?" Mavis asked, poking through them.

"This is research for my new best seller," said Daniel, beaming.

"George Orwell, Mark Twain, Lewis Carroll, Kurt Vonnegut, Joseph Heller, Oscar Wilde, Jonathan Swift, Dickens, Poe, Laurence Stern, Cervantes, Voltaire, Geoffrey Chaucer…" said Mavis, checking them out.

"You see the connection, right?" asked Daniel, looking like he had a secret no one else knew about.

"Of course. They're all well-known satirists."

"Exactly," said Daniel. "All of them a literary classic. Did you know that literary satire goes way back through the Greeks to the early literature of the Egyptians?"

"Of course, Daniel," Mavis said and chuckled, "I'm a librarian. If you're going back that far, I'm surprised that you didn't include Aristophanes in your list."

"You know your stuff, Mavis. As always. Actually, I did look for Aristophanes. Couldn't find him." Daniel grinned at her. She squinted at his cheery, almost rabid, smile.

"No, we're all out of Aristophanes, I'm afraid. There was a run on all his titles."

"Really?" Daniel said, his eyes round and wide with surprise.

"No, of course not. I was being satirical." The elderly librarian laughed.

"Oh. Nice one." Daniel laughed along with Mavis. They grinned at each other. Then the face of Daniel's friend grew quite serious. She pursed her lips and frowned with concern.

"Have you thought this through, Daniel? I didn't think satire was your thing. You're not exactly known for your sense of humor... at least among your fan base."

"Well, that's just it, Mavis. I shall be writing under a nom de plume and, as you know, being a librarian and all, that not all satire is humorous. In fact, most satire is biting, ironic and very often harsh. Some would say that the true use of satire is to provoke controversy, to stir up the populace from their torpid slumber and sound a wake-up call, challenging the status quo."

Mavis smiled gently at her young buddy. He was obviously excited about this new creative work; his enthusiasm beyond anything she had observed in a good long while.

"My, my, Daniel, I admire your chutzpah. I have no doubt that you have oceans of pent up harsh and biting criticisms of the state of the world boiling just below the surface, waiting to be unleashed. What's your topic?"

"The Guswhite book."

"*Take Control of Your life*? Why that one?"

"You were the one that said that the book was ripe for parody and satire."

"I think what I said was, it would give you a good laugh, Daniel."

"Exactly. You also said that this book and others like it are true indications that people and society are in serious trouble and... pain, remember? Lives of quiet desperation and all that? Oh, I just thought of something cool. Books like the Guswhite book are akin to the canary in the coal mine. You know how miners would take a caged canary into the coal mine and if the bird died, they knew that there were dangerous gases down there? Of course, you know that. You're a librarian." Daniel winked, hoping that she would pick up on his sarcasm. Mavis couldn't help but grin.

"Well, I can see that you're getting the hang of this satire business. I have every certainty that whatever you write will become an instant classic." Mavis efficiently put the books through the library's electronic check-out process.

"I appreciate your support, Mavis, I really do." Daniel took the large number of books and, with a final smile, and a cheery wave to his friend, he exited the library.

In the stifling hot midday sun, Daniel attracted some odd glances as he laboriously and somewhat comically, carried the large pile of books back to his studio apartment. Clumsily closing the door behind him with his left foot, he finally lost his grip and all the books spilled to the floor. Leaving them exactly where they lay, he picked up the first one from the pile, sat down in his worn and tattered armchair and began reading at page one.

He didn't want to admit it but Mavis did have a point: he was not known for his satiric sensibility. However, his plan was to read enough classic books in the genre so that he would give his mind a chance to comprehend the conventions the masters used. Then hopefully, as if by mental osmosis, he would subconsciously develop a satiric style and sensibility which he could call his own.

He checked his timepiece and knew that he would have to read as fast as he could. Not only was time of the utmost essence in a publishing sense but, because he could not afford to have his power switched back on, in a few hours he would have lost the natural light required to see the words on the page. He did have a few candles left, in various stages of helpfulness, but he wanted to keep their use to a minimum until he could buy some more. The dollar store where he usually bought them was a good pedestrian trek from his apartment. The urgency of his new project meant that he wanted to keep time-wasting trips - forays into the outside world - to a bare minimum. Researching and writing his pseudonymous satirical work, as quickly as possible, was his top priority.

Daniel read and read and read. By day, he sat in his armchair and read through the pile of books as fast as he could. As the sun slowly fell in the sky, he would move his chair closer and closer to the window to try and capture the fading natural light. Only when he couldn't read the print before him would he light a solitary candle. Then he would position the book at the proper distance and angle from the golden light in order to maximize the book's exposure to its flickering glare. Taking only bathroom breaks, he ate *in situ*. Not that he had very much to eat. He was slowly going through the contents of his small fridge and freezer, eating foodstuffs in the order with which they were spoiling from being deprived of refrigeration.

He barely slept. He was getting little sleep not because he refused to go to bed, but because when he did put himself to bed, sleep just would not come. It was the same routine, every night: he'd lie in bed, close his eyes but his manic brain just wouldn't shut off and the constant worry and chatter of his internal thoughts were beginning to drive him round the bend. What if the book wasn't a success? What if he got thrown out onto the street for non-payment of rent? What if he really did starve to death?

His father dead, his mother lived frugally in retirement in Florida; there was no way he could show up there and crash on her sofa. She had so little money for herself; there was no notion in his mind that she could in any way bail him out; she could not contribute even the slightest amount.

Apart from Mavis, he didn't have any friends. He never asked Mavis but he was pretty sure that she was volunteering at the library and wasn't even paid.

He brooded to himself. His worry was not unnecessary, unwarranted or in any way neurotic or paranoid. He was putting all his stock into the acceptance, publication and success of a book he had yet to write. It was a satire, at that; a genre as foreign to him as a thriller, mystery or romance. Perhaps I should write one of those, after all, he considered.

His lack of restorative, stage four sleep, coupled with his malnutrition and his exceedingly high stress levels didn't auger well for the writing of a modern-day best-seller (not to mention a perennial classic, a book following in the great tradition of literary masterpieces) but he was going to give it his best shot. He had to constantly remind himself that what he was endeavoring to achieve could be done and that many artists before him - a list too long to even contemplate - produced some of their best work under similar or even greater hardship.

Daniel's transition from researching the manuscript to writing the tome happened so smoothly and subtly that he would have been hard pressed to name the date that he began to write. For many days, he was engaged in obsessive research and the final day of research bled into a period of writing his satirical masterpiece.

Daniel didn't know exactly how long it took him to write the book; time seemed to be passing by in one long, continuous manic blur. Just like a gambler in a Las Vegas casino, who has stayed too long and didn't own a watch, it was impossible for him to know what the actual time was nor even to discern whether the hour was in the AM or the PM. Daniel gave up the routine of going to bed at a certain hour each evening; the only actual rest he got was when his eyes involuntarily closed due to the inability to keep them open any longer.

Daniel wrote around the clock, taking breaks only for bathroom business and the obligatory charging of his laptop. Devoid of power in his apartment, Daniel would periodically sneak out and plug his laptop into an unused outlet in one of the hallways in the building. There he would remain, writing frantically until his laptop regained its full charge. He was oblivious to dust bunnies, passersby, and the odd cockroach which wandered past. In a waking dream state, he didn't know if he wrote the book in days or in weeks. Yet finish it he eventually did. He was rather pleased with the result.

Some of the passages flowed so naturally and effortlessly, his fingers could barely keep up with his thought processes and he had typed at a feverish pace. He made numerous typos in the process but he knew that he could easily correct any typographical errors in the proofreading stage. He knew that some parts of the book were really good as they had made him laugh out loud whilst he was typing, something that he had never experienced before.

It was moments of flow that he loved so much and he became quite energized as he acted as a conduit to their passing. On those occasions, he felt like the ideas were coming from someplace else and that he was transcribing the fully-formed thoughts and ideas rather than being their originator or creator. At some frenzied moments, he didn't even know what words he was typing and could just barely make out the ideas and concepts.

The entire writing experience was like one he had never experienced before and he would be at a loss in knowing how to or in trying to replicate it. He had read of other authors who, in talking about their writing process, described such styles of writing. They would make statements that in their opinion, the writing came from the muses or the universe or the divine, or some ineffable "other." Whatever words they used to describe the experience, the concept remained consistent: they felt that they had to get out of the way of the creativity and allow the knowledge and the intuitive concepts to flow through.

Now, for the first time in his life, he felt like he understood what they had been describing. In terms of lateralization of the brain, it was the resting of the dominance of the controlling, analytical, logical and ordered left hemisphere of the brain which allowed the more intuitive and impulsive, visual and spatial, right hemisphere to predominate.

In any event, he was very pleased with the result of his creative process. Mavis allowed him to print out the manuscript at the library, free of charge, although he did tell her that he would be repaying her kindness many times over in the not-too-distant future.

YOU HAVE A BRAIN – USE IT!

Suzanne sat comfortably in her Beverly Hills adjacent plush corner office which provided a generous fourth floor view of busy Wilshire Boulevard. With a pained and puzzled facial expression, she leafed through Daniel's manuscript like it was either unreadable or written in some arcane language or code which was indecipherable to her. Her office phone buzzed. Dropping the manuscript she punched her phone.

"Yeah?" she asked and rubbed her neck and shoulders as if the read had physically hurt her.

"It's Daniel Waterstone on line one. Are you in a meeting?" Darlene, the receptionist, asked via speakerphone.

"No, I'll talk to him. Thanks, Darlene." Suzanne pressed a button on the phone. "Daniel," she greeted him brightly. "What's goin' on?"

"Hey, Suzanne. I'm calling to make certain that you received my latest work," said Daniel, trying to sound collected and calm, and entirely together, in an effort to mask his extreme apprehension and nervousness.

"Yeah, it's right here," said Suzanne, not sure how to give voice to her puzzlement. "*You Have a Brain – Use it!* by Charles Spectrum," she said in a curious tone. "I'm assuming that you're Charles Spectrum and you actually wrote this... manuscript, yeah?"

"I know. I've sold out and gone commercial," Daniel said jokingly and laughed nervously. "Can't beat them, join them, right?"

"Not sure who're you joining, Daniel but this book... it's such a departure for you. I'm not sure where to start."

Suzanne fell silent.

"Have you read it?" asked Daniel, the muscles of his body tightening in expectation of a negative verdict.

"No, I haven't read it yet," answered Suzanne. "It just got to my desk. I'll tell you what, leave it with me and I'll get back to you, how's that?"

"Sounds good to me," said Daniel, secretly squirming. His best case scenario was that she would have told him that she loved it and it was amazing, just what the market was crying out for, right now. "How long do you think..?"

Suzanne hung up on Daniel, not purposefully cutting him off, exactly. She was in a hurry to go and urgently felt the need to move to the next item on her calendar. As far as she was concerned, the book was a puzzle and she really didn't have the time to try to sort it out. As Suzanne leafed some more through the manuscript, reading passages at random, her assistant, Sidney entered to retrieve the recyclables, which he religiously did, once a week.

Once again, Sidney was not at all surprised to see that, unlike most people working in the offices, Suzanne did not at all care to separate her recyclables from her trash. Hence, presumably, she was yet another agent who didn't have much environmental concern for the planet.

"Suzanne, it doesn't take a second to decide which bin is for trash and which is for recycling," said Sidney, his hands practically on his hips. Care for the environment was of paramount concern to Sidney and many others on the staff, particularly the younger assistants and interns. He did not care if it was annoying to his boss; the future of the planet itself was at stake. He would remind her, as often as necessary, of her ecological negligence.

"Paper goes in the green container and all other trash goes in the black trash can," Sidney said, retrieving everything from the green container that didn't belong.

"Paper here, all other trash in here," he demonstrated, hoping at long last to make his point.

"Here," said Suzanne, annoyed with Daniel's unwieldy and indecipherable manuscript as much or more than she was agitated by Sidney. "Trash." Suzanne threw the manuscript at him, hitting him in the neck and head; his spectacles sent flying through the air.

"Suzanne!" reprimanded Sidney in a tone which carried no bite.

Oblivious, Suzanne got on the phone to make a call. Sidney replaced his spectacles and picked up the manuscript from the floor. *You Have a Brain—Use it!* By Charles Spectrum, he read, the title catching his eye and arousing his curiosity immediately. He leafed through it.

§

Daniel literally sat by his home phone waiting for it to ring. He didn't know what else to do with himself. He had put all the reserve he had into this one last gamble of the publishing dice. As he sat there, practically glaring at the phone, willing it to ring, his emotions ran the gamut from joyous excitement to abject fear and panic.

It's a slam dunk, he thought to himself. It's taking so long because Suzanne was bargaining, negotiating with several publishers who all want the title. She's playing one against the other, pushing up the price until she gets what she wants. She's a master at what she does; it's all good and the advance was going to be huge. What if everyone has rejected it and it's free-falling, all the way down from the top tier publishers to the small and independent presses? Then his attitude would flip 180 degrees.

It's taking so long because she can't get any takers and she was practically begging her contacts to read it, pulling in favors that she'll have to repay in the future? She hasn't read it. It's at the bottom of a slush pile with all of the unopened unsolicited submissions which will get tossed into the recycling bin, shredded or returned to the author.

The uncertainty of the situation, which was fraught with tension, made it impossible for him to function. His insomnia intensified. He grew as thin and lean as a yoga guru, not eating, pacing his tiny place, sweating in the summer heat of Los Angeles.

As the days turned into weeks, Daniel resolved himself to what he considered to be the reality of the situation: he would never sell another book for the rest of his life, and, as a consequence, he was done, finished, kaput. It was the end of line for him.

Even forgetting about the brain book, which was now a total embarrassment to him, so much so that Daniel knew that he couldn't telephone Suzanne ever again or mention the manuscript to anybody, his career was over. Thank heavens, he thought, that any evidence of the manuscript didn't get put up on the internet, either as a logline, summary or title or as a work in progress. Not that he would have put it up there as he purposefully avoided any internet presence, period. He had no personal or author website, nor did he open a Twitter, Facebook or any other social networking account. He considered himself to be a man-of-letters and not a man of blog posts or tweets. In fact, he wasn't even sure he knew what a tweet was. He had heard the word, though, and there was something more than a little obscene about it.

Perhaps his adherence to anonymity actually hurt him in this anything-you-need-to-know-about-anything-is-on-the-internet age? Suzanne had advised him on many, many occasions that it was in his professional interest, as an author, to create high visibility on the internet as a way of becoming established and building up a fan base. "Blog and build a web-based author platform to engage with fans, other authors, book promoters and readers of books," Suzanne had admonished Daniel. He had recoiled in revulsion at the thought. What on earth would Herman Melville or Thomas Wolfe tweet about, he wondered? What would Langston Hughes, Emily Dickinson or Nathaniel Hawthorne put up on their Facebook pages?

Had Suzanne been right? *Was* he too principled and elitist not to even have considered it? The work should speak for itself, he had told her pointedly. He had believed that he should not have to become a small-time peddler of his work. Trying to sell himself on the internet was not so far removed from going door-to-door with a suitcase full of his books, trying to interest apathetic homesteaders in buying his manuscripts; please, buy two and the third one is free. He shuddered to think of it. It's akin to hustling or worse, begging, he had said. Then he had added that he'd rather starve than reduce his standards to such low levels.

And, as he had inadvertently suggested he would rather do, here he was, starving: not metaphorically starving, but actually so; as in, he had not ingested any real food for some time, starving. He didn't know when he had eaten last. He vaguely remembered the gratitude he felt some weeks past in finding an old pack of ramen noodles that had obviously fallen behind his food cabinet at some point. He had ignored the fact that some cockroaches or other bugs might have crawled over the torn opening in the plastic wrapper and regardless, he duly soaked the noodles in cold water and ate them ravenously, as soon as they had softened.

There were other concerns, equally as serious, as his failure to eat regularly or at all in the recent past. He had received several 'pay or quit' notices from his landlord; he was unsure just how many. He was aware that, perhaps, he should be concerned about receiving a thumping knock on his door from the sheriff and his posse at any minute. Eviction was likely eminent, yet the truth of the situation was that he did not care. He didn't quite know at what exact moment that he had stopped caring. It wasn't a conscious decision. It was not as if he had said to himself: "I'll stop caring, now, thank you very much." The decision just seemed to get made, all by itself. At one point he cared. Then he did not.

He was also vaguely aware that he was not quite himself; certainly not at the top of his game, mentally or otherwise. The continued and perpetual stress had taken its toll. Additionally, his incessant lack of sleep and severe lack of nutrition had transformed him. In short, he was a total mess, both physically and mentally. He hadn't weighed himself lately but looking at himself in the mirror earlier that day shocked him. He looked just skin and bone, not too dissimilar from photographs he had seen of concentration camp survivors.

How did things get to be this way, he wondered. Life had been trundling along, and then things... became a blur. Yet he was unsure exactly of the events and of the time progression which had brought him to this moment in time. At some juncture, his mind had obviously entered a brain fog but he couldn't pin it down to a particular event or instant in time.

Perhaps the fog had begun like an unobtrusive and harmless mist, seemingly innocuous and benign. It obviously hadn't given cause for any mental alarm bells to sound. Obviously, the mist then slowly and gradually thickened, until it became so dense that his clear mental thought had become impaired. His clarity of thought must have gradually been replaced with the mental equivalent of brain soup.

Just like a frog placed in cold water, which was then very gradually heated, no alarm bells went off in the frog's brain. Then it was too late: the frog was cooked. It was now someone's dinner. Daniel's brain seemed similarly deceived.

Naturally, my thinking and reasoning faculties were impaired, he thought to himself. Then he wondered if such impairment had impacted or affected his will in any way, because he didn't seem to have any. It wasn't as if he had decided that he wanted to starve himself to the point that he would drift off to sleep and subsequently shuffle off his mortal coil. He had simply reached a threshold of not caring. Let sleep come, let the sheriff come, let the floods come or a plague of locusts, or any myriad number of travesties or tragedies come. He didn't or, perhaps more accurately, couldn't care.

If he did have something like a concern center in his brain (a dedicated area that sounded alarm bells to the rest of the system when something wasn't quite right and needed attention), then it was on the fritz. The neurons in that area were not firing, as they should. That part of his brain was quite plainly, in no uncertain terms, out of order. And it was the calmest, most sublime feeling that he had ever experienced in his life: no stress, no worries, no pressure to do something with or without urgency, no second-guessing what he should be doing or what he should be writing; no anxious thoughts or fear of what tomorrow may bring. There was only the present moment. It felt like... bliss.

Not that the present moment was in any way special or spectacular, it wasn't. It was just the present and it was new. He had never been solely aware of and in the present before, without the intrusion of fearful thoughts, or the voice of his conscience, or of any other kind of mental prodding, urging him on or judging him for his laziness or his inactivity or his self-pity. He felt free of his own self-imposed grief and yet, at the same time, a prisoner of his circumstance.

As pleasant and benign as this mental state of non-doing and non-thinking was, he wasn't sure if he could shift himself out of it. Could he even muster the energy and motivation to do so? Is this how a sick animal dies, he wondered. He had read of how a wounded dog, for instance, would find a spot beneath a table, or in a corner somewhere, where it could lie peacefully, and prepare itself for the sleep of death. Was that what was happening? Would he soon close his eyes to sleep and not wake up?

Would I be missed, he asked himself. No doubt his mother would grieve but she would soon return to her own concerns. It wasn't as if his disappearance from the world would disrupt her life in any big way. She would probably repeat what she had already been saying since he was a small child: what a tragedy that our boy had such unfulfilled potential.

Would Daniel miss being in the world? His first thought was, no, that he would not. He had never truly felt a part of the world in the first place. Perhaps it was because he was home-schooled and kept at home with his parents so much that he felt sheltered from other kids and people growing up. His TV viewing was so restricted that, perhaps, he had missed out on an essential cultural education with which the rest of his generation was growing up with.

He wasn't allowed to play sports for fear that he would injure himself. His exposure to other neighborhood kids was so slight that, not only did he never have a best friend growing up, he never had any friends, at all. Even when he got to play with other boys his age, he had a hard time relating. He didn't understand their enthusiasm for collecting baseball cards, for instance. Less logical was their penchant for downloading rock and pop songs, which not only sounded trite to his ears but also so similar, that it was as if they were listening to the same song over and over except they had been recorded by different artists.

But what he especially didn't understand was why other boys were so negative, spiteful, aggressive, competitive and so swift to act with violence. Of all his childhood memories which concerned other children, it was the violent encounters that remained fresh in his mind. It was those occasions as a young boy, where he was mocked, bullied, punched, kicked, spat on, called derogatory names, pushed around and generally mistreated, which maintained prominence in his memory. Sorrowful memories were disproportionately memorable, compared to recollections of good times.

The behavior of adults, in his experience, was not too far removed from the aggressive acts of neighborhood children. Any edition of the evening news on TV demonstrated that fact very well. When he was allowed to watch current event and news programs, he remembered his outright shock. Murders, stabbings, riots, violent demonstrations, wars, thefts, rapes, burglaries, corruption, abductions, destruction of property, robberies, shootings... the list went on. The world at large seemed to be in a constant state of madness and mayhem, a continuous stream of craziness born with the beginning of humanity and continuing, sadly, with no end in sight.

Violence being something which he could not relate to, he didn't understand the world then nor grow to understand it even as he matured into adulthood and developed his reason and intellect. He never did feel like he belonged on the planet or even that he was a full, card-carrying member of the human race.

As a kid, he sometimes entertained thoughts that he

was actually an alien that was either purposefully or mistakenly delivered to a human family that was raising him up as one of their own. At some point, he reasoned, the mistake would be discovered or perhaps his secret mission would end. Then, his authentic, alien family, the kin that was like him, would come rescue him and take him back to his people.

There would probably be a big celebration and he would laugh and regale the other aliens with tales of his exploits among the humans. They would have a hard time understanding, he reasoned. It was one of those, "you really had to be there" kind of things but perhaps he could write stories about his adventures in this strange world and pass it off as science fiction.

Daniel's thoughts came back to the present moment. For the first time; he wondered why he was lying stretched out on the floor and not sitting in his armchair or resting on his bed. Did I fall or just lie down where I stood? As he looked up and out through the open slits of the venetian blinds, he could see that the sun had fallen from the heavens and that the moon was beginning to exert its dominance in the dark evening sky.

Indeed, the moon was almost full and cast a blue-grey light on the drifting baby clouds which surrounded its distant orbit. Some dancing branches, from the birch tree just outside, cast morbid shadows on the window. Daniel found the imagery and movement soothing and quite hypnotic. As he mindlessly watched the random movement of the shadow branches, Daniel's eyes slowly and surely began to close.

MEET MR. CHARLES SPECTRUM

Ring-ring. Daniel's home phone rang. Without an answering machine to stop its clamor, and connect the caller to voicemail, the old style phone continued to ring loudly. Ring-ring. It was early morning. The sun beamed its life-giving rays through the window and cast a golden hue on Daniel's sleeping body which was still sprawled out on the carpeted floor.

Ring-ring. Daniel's eyes slowly opened. Ring-ring. After a quick adjustment to the morning light, they lazily settled on the ringing telephone which sat on a small table beside his cozy armchair. The phone finally stopped ringing. Still disoriented from his deep slumber, Daniel raised himself up into a seated position.

Ring-ring. The phone rang again.

This time, Daniel stared at the phone as if he couldn't believe what he was hearing; in fact, he was sure he was hallucinating. Just to make sure, he leaned forward and placed his left ear closer to the ringing phone just to see if the noise got louder as the result of his proximity. Strangely, it did. Ring-ring. As the phone continued to ring, he slowly stretched out his hand and with deliberate caution, lifted the handset from its cradle. Very carefully, he raised it to his ear and listened. There was silence at first but then he heard a voice.

"Hello?" a woman's voice said.

"Hello?" he uncertainly answered back.

"Daniel?" the voice asked.

"Yes?"

"It's Suzanne."

Daniel still doubted the reality of the encounter and was not discounting that he may yet be hallucinating the entire experience. "That's impossible," said Daniel.

"What are you talking about?" asked Suzanne. "What's impossible?"

"They cut the phone off weeks ago," said Daniel, pretty sure of his facts.

"I know. I paid your bill."

"You did?"

"Daniel, listen to me," Suzanne started, as if she didn't have much time. "Your book? The one about using your brain?"

"Oh, yeah," said Daniel in an embarrassed and apologetic tone. "I know. I'm sorry about that..."

"Sidney, my assistant, reads it and he liked it and started showing it around to the other interns. Anyway, suddenly the whole office was making copies and they were sending it to their friends. So, with all the buzz, I sent it over to Bubbleday..."

Suzanne was talking so fast that Daniel's brain was not assimilating a great deal of what she was saying. In fact, his brain was still trying to process what it meant that Suzanne had paid his bill and had his phone switched back on.

"They put it into print right away and guess what? It's a hit! I think you hit the jackpot with this one!" Suzanne paused in her excitement and, quite obviously, expected an equally excited response. When all she heard was silence on the other end, she wondered if the call had gotten cut off. "Daniel?" she asked. "Are you still there?"

"Yes, I'm here," said Daniel.

"Did you hear what I said? Bubbleday published your book! I've been trying to get a hold of you for weeks but I didn't have your address, only this phone number that didn't seem to be a working number for the longest while...

Isn't that great news?"

"Yes," said Daniel, still mentally out of it. "Did they send a check?"

"You betcha," exclaimed Suzanne. "Can you come into the office and pick it up?"

"I could swing by," said Daniel.

It was some time after Daniel returned the handset to the cradle that the penny eventually dropped. The book got published. The book got published. Daniel mentally repeated the sentence to himself, over and over again, as if, by repeating it to himself, he would eventually understand. The more he repeated it to himself, the more indeed it actually began to make sense to him. The book which he wrote in a frenzy, under a different name, was now in print. He had some money coming to him; he just needed to get himself over the hill to Suzanne's office to pick it up and hopefully get some groceries and pay some bills. Perhaps the check would be big enough to have the power switched back on.

As his mind started ticking over, elements of his reality and putting who he was into context (generally noting what he was and had been doing and thus where he stood in the world), he felt that he was coming back into himself more and more. Things began to feel more real; he actually felt his backside connecting with the armchair that he was sitting in.

His vision got sharper. Looking around his apartment, he noticed how dirty and unkempt it was. There were stains on the carpet that he didn't remember being there before. There was trash on the floor, rolled up note paper mostly (probably from taking notes from books and some scribbled down story-ideas, from brain-storming sessions, he decided).

He could feel his feet on the floor and was now aware

of his blood circulating through his veins. Along with his body, he felt his brain waking up again; his thoughts were becoming sharper. He needed to devise a plan of action. He had something to do now, a place to go. He was being reprieved, at least for a little while, a few more days, perhaps; maybe a couple of weeks, if the amount of money was large enough.

He would need to get cleaned up and change into some clean clothes, if he had any. When he looked in the bathroom mirror he was surprised to see that he had a beard. It was a pretty decent one, too, which for some reason, made him feel a little bit proud. His hair was long and scraggy and very dirty. He had a thought that this was how Robinson Crusoe must have looked. I look like I was marooned on an uninhabited and desolate island, he pondered. Except Daniel's island had been his own apartment, as uninhabited and as desolate as living in a big city can be, ironically enough.

Thank heavens the water is still running, he thought to himself when he turned the water tap on, even if it was cold only. Braving the cold running water, and soaping himself all over, Daniel experienced a brief moment of glee. At least he could get clean.

Showered and dressed, Daniel searched for and eventually found a pair of scissors. He began the task of cutting his hair and beard and generally cleaning himself up in order to look somewhat decent and presentable for his trek to the tony mid-Wilshire district. Rifling through his coin jar, he was relieved to find enough silver coins to cover his bus fare plus a transfer, if it was so needed. Perhaps this is the beginning of act two of my publishing life, he thought to himself and smiled.

§

Daniel felt scruffy and underdressed once he entered his agent's bright and swanky office building on Wilshire Boulevard. As he sheepishly approached the quiet reception area, Darlene, the receptionist, at first gave him a cold look. Then, as she looked closer at him, her countenance brightened and she smiled broadly at him.

"I'm here to see Suzanne," Daniel said meekly. "My name is..."

"I know who you are," Darlene beamed as she pressed a button to connect with Suzanne's office. "Charles Spectrum is here for you, Suzanne. Shall I send him up?"

Daniel turned his head to see who else was waiting to see Suzanne but quickly realized that it was he that she was referring to. Then he remembered his nom de plume. It seemed so foreign, if not a little comical, to him now.

"Suzanne is coming down to get you," said a smiling and courteous Darlene. "You can take a seat, if you like. She won't be long."

"Oh, thank you," said Daniel, retreating to a black leather armchair. As Daniel waited, he wondered if he should be finding himself a decent magazine to read among the stack scattered across the coffee table. He recalled that on several visits previously, Suzanne had left him waiting in reception for quite some time. From the dusty corners of his memory, he recalled how, on one particular occasion, he was kept waiting for a whopping seventy minutes before she appeared, all smiles and with little apology.

As Daniel settled in to read an old copy of National Geographic, he couldn't help but notice that Darlene kept stealing glances at him. When he looked her way, she would quickly and rather coyly, look away again. Or perhaps he was imagining it. A moment later, the elevator doors opened to reveal an effervescent Suzanne. Looking directly at Daniel, she extended her arms wide, "Daniel." She said his name with such warmth and enthusiasm that it scared him.

He wasn't sure if her open arms were intended as an invitation for a hug but she had never hugged him before, so he played it safe by extending his hand for a friendly, yet business-like handshake. She took his hand in both of her own hands and stopped before him, as if taking him all in, as a good friend might if they had not seen someone whom they cherished in quite some time.

"How are you?" she asked in a tone that was way more meaningful than a trite greeting.

"Well," said Daniel, awkwardly. "I'm well. You?"

"You've been quite the talk around here for some time now. I'm sure your ears were burning."

"Not so much," replied Daniel, no idea what she was talking about.

"Of course, people around here know you as Charles Spectrum. I guess you'll have to start getting used to that," Suzanne said as she walked him towards the elevators. Darlene still seemed very interested in trying to catch Daniel's eye as he passed, as much as she could get away with. As he passed her desk, she leaned forward and looking like she was plucking up some courage, she managed to maintain eye-contact without looking away when their eyes met.

"I just want to say that I really, really love your book," she said, nervously.

Daniel was about to ask her which one she was referring to but Suzanne kept walking. He didn't want to get Darlene into trouble by stopping to chat.

"Thank you very much," he said, gratefully. "That means a lot."

"You're going to have to get used to that... a lot,"

Suzanne said to him as they got into the elevator.

"Hold the doors," a voice said. Suzanne pretended to press the hold button as a very attractive woman in her twenties rushed to the doors. As the doors continued to close, Daniel caught sight of the woman and was immediately smitten. He reflexively reached out his hand to wedge it between the sliding elevator doors. The doors hit his hand and immediately bounced opened again, allowing the woman to enter.

"Thank you so much," she smiled to Daniel. "I'm late for a meeting. The parking lot was full."

Daniel stared at the woman, as if he couldn't help himself. There was something about her that was captivating to him; something that he doesn't usually see in people, normally. She seemed so open and fresh and innocent. It wasn't until she looked back at him and smiled that he realized that he had been staring at her beyond what was considered socially acceptable. He suddenly panicked, his bashful eyes darting towards the floor as his face blushed bright crimson. Suzanne watched the interaction and smirked to herself.

"Clare Peterson," Suzanne said as the woman exited the elevator on the third floor. "She's a very talented composer. We represent her for movie soundtracks."

"She looks familiar," Daniel said as a cover for his inappropriate leering. "She looks like someone I know." In actual fact, Daniel was in some way correct, although her resemblance to "Crazy" Mary wasn't consciously registering with him. Despite her apparent craziness, Daniel had harbored an attraction to Mary Prendergast all during college; an attraction he never allowed himself to pursue because of her apparent differences to him as well as what he viewed as their clashing beliefs and irreconcilable opposing core life philosophies.

"Come meet the staff," Suzanne said as she lead him into the large office filled with tiny cubicles teeming with assistants and interns; the walls lined with desks for whoever was on the next rung up along the chain of command. Sidney was the first to approach Daniel and, in an extremely reverential demeanor, extended his hand towards him.

"Mr. Spectrum, your book changed my life," he said with profound meaning. "Thank you."

"Oh, you're very welcome," Daniel said, shocked upon hearing the very words he'd been wanting and waiting to hear his entire writing life. "Thank *you*."

The entire staff then stopped what they were doing and, all facing Daniel, broke into spontaneous and heartfelt applause. Shocked and speechless, Daniel briefly considered that this was all a dream. Alternatively, if he really was awake, then someone was obviously playing a practical joke and, a la *Candid Camera*, he was being punked. As the applause died down, Sidney again stepped forward. "I don't know if Suzanne has told you but, on our lunch break, we've formed a Charles Spectrum study group,"

"Oh, uh..." Daniel muttered, unable to respond and looking to Suzanne for guidance or at least some semblance of a clue as to what exactly was going on. Suzanne, however, had stepped back and was watching the entire interaction with self-satisfied amusement.

"We would be honored if you could say just a few words," continued Sidney.

Daniel was still waiting for the prank to be revealed. As he looked around at all the expectant faces, he considered that if this *was* all a gag, it was a very elaborate joke and, all things considered, not very funny. Daniel again looked to Suzanne for some support or guidance but she merely gestured for him to continue. "Well, I... I guess the uh, the main thing is to live a good life," Daniel said, half expecting them to laugh and reveal their conspiracy.

They remained quiet, however, as if expecting to hear more. Daniel tried to remember what he had written in the brain book, as obviously, the wisdom that they wanted to hear was along that same thought trajectory.

"Uh, try to use as much of your brain capacity as you possibly can and um... get to bed before midnight." As the staff once again applauded, Daniel looked almost pleadingly at Suzanne to come to his rescue.

"Okay, gang," Suzanne finally said, stepping forward, "time to get back on the phones. Charles, we've got work to do."

"A Charles Spectrum study group?" Daniel exclaimed as they entered the privacy of Suzanne's office. "What exactly is all this about, Suzanne?"

Suzanne handed Daniel the latest Bubbleday publishing catalogue. "Your book is climbing the charts is what's going on," said Suzanne as Daniel scanned the catalogue looking for categorical proof that his book had been, indeed, published.

"I don't see it," said Daniel, beginning to doubt the whole story. "The book isn't listed."

"Page seven," said Suzanne, causing Daniel to race to the page.

"Wait a minute," Daniel said.

"You still don't see it?"

"Yes, it's here. I see it. But it's listed in non-fiction under Self-Help and Personal Transformation?"

"So?"

"The book is a satire!"

"A what?"

"Satire. A literary work that exposes human follies through irony, ridicule and derision."

"It's a "how to" book, right? It's got all these exercises to reprogram the brain. Yeah?"

As if in shock, Daniel sat in the nearest chair. He felt totally flummoxed.

"It's a comedy," Daniel said calmly. "It should be listed in the humor section. I expected people would read it and, like all good satire, be able to laugh at themselves and at the ridiculousness of the human condition."

"Cheer up, Daniel. It's selling like hot cakes."

"It's selling to people who believe that by doing incredibly stupid exercises, they're going to increase their brain power. I mean, the exercises were so exaggerated... how could anyone in their right mind take them seriously? This is a travesty."

Larry, a young intern knocked on Suzanne's open door.

"Suzanne, I need today's figures," he said, sounding as someone with cerebral palsy might sound. He was using just the left side of his mouth to speak.

"You can take them, Larry. I'm finished with them," said Suzanne.

As Larry hopped into the room, Daniel could see that the young man's right leg was strapped up behind him, his right arm was in sling and he wore an eye patch on his right eye. Assuming that the fellow had recently been in some hideous accident of some kind, Daniel immediately felt compassion for him. Using his one good hand, Larry grabbed the papers from Suzanne, then turned and awkwardly hopped on his left leg right back out of the room.

"Poor guy," Daniel said when Larry had left the room. "What happened to him?"

"Nothing," said Suzanne, assuming that Daniel would already have known. "He's doing one of the exercises from your book."

Daniel was at a loss to know what exactly Suzanne was referring to.

"The one where you just use one side of your body for a month?" said Suzanne, hoping to jog his memory. "Then you switch to the other side for two months?"

Daniel was aghast. "This is exactly what I'm talking about! Can't you see how crazy that is?"

"Hey," said Suzanne, raising her palms in a gesture of surrender. "I was the first one that called the whole thing crazy, believe me. I've been decades in this business and I'm still continually surprised at the crazy shit that people buy. No offence."

"None taken."

"Never saw the whole zombie and vampire craze coming, either. You want to talk crazy?"

"Well, look," said Daniel, returning the catalogue. "You need to notify the publishers and call this whole thing off before it gets out of hand. If they relist it as satire and it doesn't sell, then so be it. The world is quite obviously in a much more perilous state than I had imagined. There is no need to further add to its craziness."

"You want to sign here for your check?" Suzanne said as she held out a check and placed some legal papers before him. "Sign here, here and here," she said, turning pages on what looked like a legal contract.

Daniel signed and then casually glanced at the check. Seeing the number of zeroes, his eyes nearly popped out of his head. He stood in a motionless pose for a few seconds, his fully opened eyes unblinking, staring at his name on a check that had so many zeroes, his brain couldn't compute. Suzanne allowed herself a smirk.

"I told you that the book is selling," she said smugly. "Crazy people buy books, I guess. And that's just print. Digital downloads is a whole other box of rainbow colored crayons. Crazy people love their Kindles."

A knock at the door roused Daniel from his trance. Another intern, Jamal, stood at the door with his back to Suzanne.

"Yes, Jamal," Suzanne said.

"Sorry to disturb, Suzanne. I need your signature," Jamal said, his body turned so that he was actually speaking into the hallway.

"Not a problem," said Suzanne.

Jamal walked backwards into the room and smiled at Daniel as he passed. Daniel weakly smiled back. Jamal extended the papers to be signed behind his back towards Suzanne, who quickly signed them. He then turned and walked backwards out the door. Daniel enquiringly looked at Suzanne. "The exercise where you walk backwards for six weeks and sleep standing up?" she said as a question in the hope that he would recognize it.

Daniel looked long and hard at the huge check in his hands. Not only could he pay all his debts and catch up with his bills but he would have so much left over, he could probably put a down payment on a small house in the suburbs. With extreme reluctance, he held the check out for Suzanne to reclaim. "I can't take this," he said, breathing in deeply to aid his resolve. "I'd feel like I'm taking it under false pretenses."

"Don't be a sap," said Suzanne, her change of tone surprising him. "You did your job. You wrote a book. You gave it to a publisher and it's their job to put it out into the market place. You have no control over who buys your book nor is it your responsibility to decide who should buy it and who shouldn't. You do know that as soon as the last page leaves your typewriter and you hand it over to us, it's no longer yours, right?"

"Yes, but..."

"Your job is done, Daniel. As frustrating as it may be for you, and all the other authors out there, you can only watch from the sidelines as your baby grows up. In most cases, they die or, more likely, stall in infancy. In some rare cases, however, a book becomes a monster. Whether we like it or not, once it goes public, a book takes on a life of its own. Maybe it turns out exactly as you expected and wanted it to turn out. Then again; maybe not. Maybe it becomes something that no one foresaw or even intended. Lewis Carroll wrote *Alice in Wonderland* as a satire of the monarchy and of English society in general, right?"

"For the most part, I guess," agreed Daniel.

"How do you think he'd feel knowing that ever since it's been considered solely as a book for children? I can hear him screaming now, "It should be listed under satire, not children's bed time stories!" People consider *Don Quixote* as a serious book but Cervantes wrote that as a satire, correct?"

Again, Daniel nodded his head in agreement. "The first major satire in modern Western literature," he agreed.

"George Orwell, *1984*. Satire, yeah? Most of Chekov's prose and plays: satire, right? I'm not just a dumb ten per center, Daniel. I did go to college. Let me give you a maxim that some of my TV clients use all the time: never underestimate your audience. Nobody in this business knows what's going to be a hit and no artist has any control over how their material is going to be perceived or interpreted once it goes out before the teeming masses. Go cash your check and buy yourself a decent meal. You sure look like you could use one."

When Suzanne finally stopped talking and sat silently at her desk, Daniel remained standing and speechless. She had surprised him with her impassioned speech and with the intelligence with which she had delivered it. Perhaps he had misperceived her, all along.

"Anything else, Daniel? I need to make some calls," Suzanne said and looked at her computer. Daniel felt faint. I need to eat, he thought.

"No," he said, rising from his chair.

"Are we good?" asked Suzanne, now smiling.

"Yeah. Yeah, we're good."

"Don't over-think it, Daniel. At the end of the day, it's just business. If they don't spend ten bucks buying your book, then they're gonna buy a book about vampires fighting wolf men with the help of goblins and elves or some shit. You're just as entitled to that ten bucks as any other author out there. Now, go get a decent haircut and eat some protein and let me sell some books."

SOMEONE TO TALK TO

Daniel continued to gape at the check in his hands as he left Suzanne's office and walked towards the elevator. The hand holding the check trembled. The enormity of the moment was not lost upon him. He could use these riches to finance his heart's desire, the dream of his soul: this money would allow him to write the final book in the *Impossible Dream* trilogy. The very idea was almost foreign to him. He had not contemplated his project in quite some time. Perhaps Fitzgerald was wrong when he wrote that there are no second acts in American life because Daniel felt certain that he was surely about to embark upon one.

As Daniel pressed the button for the elevator, young Jamal walked past him carrying a box of manuscripts. He was still walking backwards. He smiled at Daniel. Daniel smiled back. Jamal bumped into another intern whom Daniel hadn't yet met. The other intern wore a blindfold and walked along the corridor, not quite touching but rather, as if trying to *sense* the wall with his back. Daniel stared and was almost appalled at the lunacy of the exercise; presumably another zany exercise from the brain book.

Daniel put his check away as the elevator doors opened and he stepped in. There were four people in the elevator, three of them were strangers. Clare Peterson stood at the rear. Daniel commanded his eyes not to look. He wanted to avoid risking another embarrassing stare. He was the first to exit when the elevator got to the lobby.

"Charles Spectrum!" a female voice called. It took Daniel a few seconds to realize that he was the person being spoken to, so he stopped and turned. Clare Peterson stood before him. She beamed a friendly smile, so full of joy, so heart-warming, that it completely melted him. "I didn't know that it was you, earlier, until they told me," she said, sounding nervous and excited at the same time. "I know that this might sound really unusual but it's like I know you," she continued. "I mean, I know I don't know you, we haven't met or anything... it's just that I feel as if I know you already."

Daniel stared at her in an exceptionally peculiar, yet transfixed way. He wasn't aware of his staring. If he had known how odd and almost comical that he looked, he would have snapped himself right out of it. Clare looked at him in a puzzled way, perhaps wondering why he was staring at her with such a curious expression, yet staying silent. "What?" she asked, her voice a little hushed, after a long moment when neither of them spoke. "Are you picking up on something, psychically?"

"Oh, no... I'm sorry," Daniel said, finally breaking out of his trance. "I was just thinking the same thing that you were. You look like someone that I know, someone that I could talk to, you know?"

Clare smiled with such joy, that she almost laughed. "I did want to talk to you, as a matter of fact. It's so weird, actually, meeting you here today."

"Why is that?" asked Daniel, not sure he was following her meaning.

"I have a problem that I think you might be able to help me with. In fact, I don't know of anyone else who could," she said, looking like she was aware that she wasn't making much sense. "Have you eaten?" she then inquired.

"Not in several weeks," he said with a straight face. Clare laughed.

"You are entirely hilarious," she said.

Not having any sisters or female friends, besides Mavis, women were always an undiscovered country for Daniel. If he was being totally honest with himself, he would have had to admit that in some way women terrified him and he couldn't be certain of exactly why that was. He did not remember being mistreated or traumatized in any way from any representatives of the opposite sex and especially not by his mother. In retrospect, the lady might have been considered a little bit on the frosty side, emotionally, yet she was a good parent.

Sure his mom was stoic and reserved. If he had considered it further, he would have noted that both of his parents could have been described as emotionally cool. They were both school teachers, as well, although, obviously, his parents' emotionally cold and distant attitudes undoubtedly had nothing to do with their professions.

It's not like Daniel had *zero* exposure to the opposite sex; he had been on a handful of dates with different women over his lifetime but he could never seem to communicate effectively with females. Without deep communication, no real or meaningful intimacy hence evolved. As a consequence, he had never had a serious relationship. Perhaps it was because he never found a potential romantic partner who shared his interests, the way that Mavis did, for instance.

Perhaps his fear of women sprang from the fact that the women he did meet, and attempt to get to know, had areas of concern which were so different to his that it took him into places of uncertainty. Those places were outside of his comfort zone and experience. He didn't have the vocabulary or skills with which to meaningfully communicate; talking with a woman about feelings and emotions, for instance.

Mavis and he never discussed anything except literature and they could usually debate and discuss for hours on end without any sense of unease; in fact, quite the contrary, he usually felt mentally excited when conversing with Mavis. Perhaps his true, ideal female was a woman with the brain of an eighty-three year old librarian in a twenty-five year old body.

As Daniel sat across from Clare, over lunch in a local Thai restaurant, the longer that their conversation progressed, the more he considered the possibility that the adorable and energetically positive woman before him could be "the one." What further confirmed his analysis was that, despite the fact that they never once discussed reading habits, writing or literature, he didn't during one moment of their togetherness feel uneasy, insecure or stressed: in fact, quite the opposite.

As she talked about herself: her childhood and her inner world growing up... well, she could have been describing Daniel, exactly. The more she spoke, the more he realized that everything she was saying was so similar to his own experience that she could have been reading entries from his own personal diary.

"All my life, I've just felt so alienated," she continued. "When I was a child, I was sure that my real family were aliens who lived on another planet and for some reason they had posted me here in this remote and backwards planet on some kind of mission that I've forgotten or had no awareness of..."

"And some day they'll return to pick you up and take you back home where everything will start to make sense and you'll get to be with your real people," Daniel said, finishing her thoughts.

"Yes!" said Clare, shocked and excited to be finally understood. "That's it exactly!"

"Me, too," said Daniel. "I've never once felt that I belong here, in this world, on this planet, among this humanity..."

"For the longest time I've felt like I can't be human, you know?"

"I know exactly," agreed Daniel.

"The concerns of everyone around me, the way people think, their priorities... I could never relate. So, I thought that it must be me, right? That I'm the alien."

"I guess you're not alone, after all," said Daniel, raising his glass in a toast.

"Nor you," Clare smiled broadly and clinked his glass.

"Where have you been all my life?" asked Daniel.

"We've made a connection, haven't we?" asked Clare, although it sounded more like a statement.

"I think we have," responded Daniel, meeting her eyes in what felt to him like a deep and soulful visual embrace.

"Can I get you two anything else?" the waiter approached, breaking their connection.

"No," said Daniel, disappointed by the interruption. "Just the check, please."

"Like I said, when I invited you to lunch, this is my treat," said Clare. "I insist."

"Fair enough," said Daniel, hiding his deep relief. "I'll get the next one."

Clare smiled at the thought. "What was the problem that you mentioned earlier?" asked Daniel. "Or was that just a ruse?" he said, smiling.

"No, no, I was serious... *am* serious about that," Clare remonstrated. "There is something that you might be able to help me with," she said softly, leaning forward.

"Absolutely," said Daniel, moving towards her and adopting her confidential demeanor.

"I want to stop levitating," Clare said, sounding serious,

if not a little distressed.

Daniel waited for her either to laugh or repeat what she really said because obviously he didn't hear her properly. When she remained quiet and expectant for a response, Daniel realized that perhaps he did hear her correctly, after all. "You did say 'levitating,' right?" asked Daniel, just to be one hundred per cent sure.

"Isn't that weird?" she asked, nervous about how he was going to respond.

"Yes," agreed Daniel calmly. "That's very weird."

"It's just at night, when I'm sleeping. Four, four-thirty in the morning, I'll wake up and I'm like three feet off of the bed."

"In mid air?" asked Daniel, again making sure that he had the facts.

"I haven't mentioned this to anyone, not even my shrink. I mean, who could I talk to? People would think that I'm nuts, right?"

"Yes, I would think so," agreed Daniel, himself trying hard not to scream, 'She's a nutcase, after all,' and running at top speed out of the restaurant.

"Then when I read your book... It's like you spoke straight to my soul, you know?" Clare continued, her eyes soft and vulnerable, perhaps even a little pleading. "It's like you walked right into my heart, opened me up and saw me for who I truly am," she said, her voice almost shaking. "And now, here I am, eating lunch with you. Making a connection," she said brightening, almost as if she couldn't believe her good fortune.

Daniel consciously projected a pensive demeanor and smiled politely, secretly wishing that the check would finally arrive. Clare raised her glass in a toast, encouraging him with her eyes to do likewise, which he did.

"Here's to two people that have been feeling so alone

all of their lives," she said gravely, her eyes tearing up, "so very, very alone."

The waiter arrived and placed the bill on Daniel's side of the table, which, considering that he was not carrying any cash, immediately spooked him. Clare quickly grabbed the check. "Don't even think about it," she said.

"Have it your way, then," Daniel said, thinking that he sounded like a gentleman. "Thank you very much for the lovely lunch."

"Are you kidding? This has been amazing. You have no idea," Clare gushed.

"Let me think about the levitating thing and I'll get back to you, how's that?" he said, tossing his napkin onto his plate and preparing to rise.

"I feel like I'm in very capable hands with you, Charles Spectrum," she said, handing him her business card. "My personal phone number is on the back."

"Cool," said Daniel, checking it out with exaggerated interest.

EVEN CRAZY PEOPLE NEED A LEADER

Daniel wasted no time in paying his debts, catching up on his bills and, for the first time in his adult life, buying himself a brand new car. As he drove the streets of Los Angeles, he would occasionally take deep and full breaths, savoring the new car smell. In fact, driving aimlessly around LA became one of his newest past times; cruising about in a brand spanking, shiny new Jetta, with no concern whatsoever for the increasingly high price of gas, made him feel downright decadent; this is a feeling, he thought to himself, that I could get used to.

Money can do strange things to a man, he thought to himself, as he drove along the Pacific Coast Highway, and watched the fiery orange-gold sun dipping below the ocean horizon on his right. He never had much disposable income before; his entire life, he had always seemed to struggle, scraping by to make the rent and utilities every month. Money had forever been an almost abstract concept to him, as if it were merely something that other people had and never something for him to aspire to having in any great amounts.

In fact, you could almost sum up the entire cannon of modern Western literature as, in some ways, a morality tale. In most cases, the texts depicted those that had it - the wealthy - as being morally vacuous or, in many cases, ethically corrupt. Those that didn't have it - the poor and hard working, lower classes - as being pure in heart, noble and morally virtuous.

He searched his brain for literary heroes that were

82

both honorable and stinking rich at the same time; he couldn't think of one. Even the great Gatsby himself, who was rich and in all ways a gentleman, was, according to Nick, the narrator, a person of questionable morals who came into his wealth in some allegedly nefarious fashion, which was never stated nor indeed proven; almost as if just because he was a very wealthy, self-made man, he had to have earned it in some devious and possibly, illegal manner.

It wasn't as if Daniel was wealthy, by any stretch of the imagination; indeed he had already blown through most of his recent windfall, but he definitely did feel a difference within himself just from having had a little taste of wealth. He noticed that he smiled more. He also stood more erect and walked with an assurance and confidence which, although it was a mostly unconscious behavior on his part, he nevertheless noticed. He slept more deeply and soundly at night, perhaps now because his fears of not making it financially seemed more distant, at least for the moment.

The more he thought about having money, the more he realized that he liked it and indeed, he would like it even better if he had some more. The thought surprised him and he smiled, almost deviously, as if he were falsely equating himself with a morally corrupt wealthy reprobate from a Charles Dickens novel. What difference would it make to him if he did have more money, he wondered. If writing was truly the only thing to him that mattered, would he become a worse writer, as a result? Perhaps he'd become a better writer?

If he had more money, instead of worrying about inconsequential financial matters, he could concentrate entirely upon his artistic work. Perhaps, like many writers before him, he could rent a room in an elegant hotel and devote his time fully to his literary pursuits without having to worry about food, cleaning or even making his own bed.

Indeed, he could decide on a whim to take his laptop off to any place in the world and, depending on his mood and subject, pen a romantic tragedy in Paris, a tale of financial greed and comeuppance in London or New York or maybe an *Old Man and The Sea* type of narrative written at a café by a beach on a quaint, yet remote island in the Mediterranean.

Having more money would not corrupt him, he decided; it would simply give him more choices in life. He could also do good deeds like give away free laptops to inner city schools where literacy among the young was a major problem. He could help out his mother and provide her with more comforts in her declining years. Boy, he'd love to see the look of pride on her face when he finally reversed the trend and he helped her out, for a change.

With more money, he could actually consider buying one or more properties and maybe live in Paris or London for six months of the year and maintain a vacation home in the South of France. Would there be a Mrs. Waterstone in the picture, he wondered to himself, feeling almost bashful for having the thought. Why not, he considered. There was no reason why he couldn't have a devoted wife along with a successful literary career, as long as she was supportive and didn't interfere with his life's work.

She would need to be certifiably sane and emotionally balanced, however, and not like that Clare woman who seemed wonderful until she began talking of her penchant for defying the forces of gravity whilst she slumbered. I dodged a bullet there, he sighed.

If there was going to be a Mrs.Waterstone, she would have to have her life in order. He couldn't constantly be at her beck and call, talking her down off the proverbial ledge every few moments. She could not be emotionally demanding like so many literary heroines from the works of the Bronte sisters and every one of Jane Austen's novels. "Low maintenance," was the modern-day term for what he needed, he reasoned: someone caring, supportive, intelligent and requiring low, low maintenance.

It was a surprise to Daniel that, within a few days, Suzanne invited him to dinner at a very swanky restaurant in Beverly Hills and made it very clear in the invitation that, as this was a business dinner, that she would be picking up the tab (or perhaps her agency, to be more precise). What was more curious to Daniel was why it was an evening meeting and not a business luncheon, which was more the accepted norm. If his agent wanted to give Daniel an update of some kind, she could update him perfectly well over the phone. If papers needed signing, a visit to her office would suffice. An evening meal in a class A expensive restaurant, that her agency was paying for, meant that it could only be good news which she had for him, Daniel mused. Perhaps they're going to publish part two of *The Impossible Dream* series, after all.

Much to Daniel's abject disappointment, all throughout dinner, Suzanne talked about everything and anything except for *The Impossible Dream* series. Despite the fact that, when she invited him, she had mentioned that she had lots of news to impart, Suzanne spoke little about business. He masticated his food carefully and listened as she babbled. When would she get to the point, he wondered. The apparent lack of substance in their meeting caused Daniel to question exactly why they were meeting in the first place. "You said that you had some news, Suzanne?" Daniel finally plucked up the courage to ask.

"All in good time, Daniel," answered Suzanne, taking another sip from the most gloriously delicious bottle of wine that he had ever tasted. She was imbibing quite a lot of wine, he noticed. Was she a bit drunk? Daniel wondered.

"I thought that tonight could be our little meet and greet meeting," she said, slurring her words a little.

"Didn't we meet and greet years ago?" asked Daniel, unsure if he was understanding the industry term very well. "We've known each other for years, right?"

"Do we, Daniel?" Suzanne asked cryptically. "Do we really know each other?"

Daniel hesitated, not knowing how to answer, as clearly they did know each other, since she was the reason he had moved to Los Angeles in the first place.

"I thought I knew you," she continued, "until you handed in the brain manuscript. Then when it took off, I realized that I don't know you at all. Who is this alter ego of yours, "Charles Spectrum," for instance? I don't know this side of you one bit."

"Oh," replied Daniel, not sure how to respond. "I'm not quite sure I know who he is, either," he said, forcing a laugh which she didn't buy or entertain.

"Seriously, Daniel. Who the frack is Charles Spectrum?" Suzanne asked pointedly, her eyes catching him in an eye hold, as if demanding a serious answer.

"I don't know, Suzanne. It was a momentary lapse of sanity on my part. I tried to write a satire, a genre I'm evidently not suited to... and this book is what came out. I'm as surprised as you are, trust me. I'm just amazingly fortunate that it has worked out for the best and offered me a reprieve. The rewards will allow me to continue writing..." Daniel stopped talking when he noticed that Suzanne was smiling unusually broadly. She looked as if she were about to break into laughter.

"Offered you a reprieve, Daniel," she said. "Is that what you think? A temporary lapse of insanity and this is the book that came out?" Suzanne repeated, her cheeks pinkening, and it was obvious that she was laughing internally.

"I don't understand," said Daniel, feeling nervous and a little embarrassed from not being privy to her private, and obviously terribly humorous, joke.

"You have no idea what you have here, do you?" she asked. Daniel shrugged.

"This book is not a reprieve or some interlude... some little bit of writerly doodling which you did in between writing your serious novels... this book is a sensation!" She spoke so loudly that the couple at an adjoining table turned their heads to investigate. "It's a best seller, a block-buster, a publishing phenomenon... a huge freaking hit!" Suzanne continued.

"I wrote the thing in a crazed frame of mind," Daniel protested. "The book is garbage."

"Only to you, Daniel. To hundreds of thousands out there, it's a gem... it's a masterpiece... a godsend."

"Hundreds of thousands, what now?" said Daniel, not understanding her correctly.

"Come with me," Suzanne said, retrieving her credit card from the restaurant bill folder. "I want to show you something."

Daniel drove his new car and followed Suzanne, thinking she was heading back to the office which was a short drive away. When Suzanne passed the turn for the office and continued driving west, Daniel wondered if he should continue to follow her; where is she going, he wondered. Has she changed her mind and decided to simply drive back home, maybe too drunk to realize that Daniel was still trailing her car. When Suzanne slowed down, instead of running through an amber traffic light, Daniel realized that she was still cognizant of his presence.

Daniel followed Suzanne through Westwood and into Brentwood, where many of the rich and famous like to reside in their leafy-strewn hide-away mansions. As Suzanne pulled off the main roads and drove through the narrower and winding side streets, Daniel began to feel more and more anxious, although he couldn't put his finger exactly on the reason why.

Turning off of the main, well-known Los Angeles thoroughfares, Daniel found himself in unfamiliar terrain. He drove along the dimly-lit streets of the rich and elite, following Suzanne, traversing a world he had previously had no access to. Perhaps this evenings excursion was an indication of his new life to be; was he finally being accepted into the upper echelons of L.A. society, where the decision-makers and arbiters of good taste - the cultured elite - held court?

Suzanne finally parked in the driveway of a medium-sized home in a quiet cul de sac. Daniel parked on the street and followed her through the front door which she had entered and left open.

"Cognac?" Suzanne asked, already at her cocktail cabinet.

"What's going on, Suzanne?" Daniel asked, looking around what appeared to be her home. "You never invited me into your home before. Why are you suddenly being so friendly to me?"

Suzanne handed Daniel a drink in a beautifully cut crystal snifter. "My world is built on relationships, Daniel. The relationship between an agent and a client is a very delicate one. If you write garbage and I encourage you, you write more garbage. If you write great stuff and I spend time with you, developing that relationship further, you write better material. This is good business practice, that's all."

"So then, you're encouraging me to write more books like the one I just wrote, which I think is junk, because you think it is... terrific material?"

"Daniel, don't get me wrong. I think your literary novels are masterpieces, which is why I've stuck with you all these years. One thing I've learned in this business is that, at the end of the day, it doesn't matter what you or I think is good or bad. What matters is what the marketplace thinks is good or bad and luckily for us, as far as the marketplace is concerned, there's no guesswork involved. If what you produce fulfils some need out there, then the people will buy it; if the market doesn't perceive any value in your work, then no one will purchase it: it's as simple as that."

Suzanne handed Daniel an envelope. "Surprise number one."

"What's this?" asked Daniel, opening the envelope as Suzanne walked into another room.

"A big fat check, made out to you, Mr. Charles Spectrum."

"But I already got a check," said Daniel.

"The book has completely sold out its first printing and is now on a second. They can't get it onto the shelves fast enough," said Suzanne from the other room. Daniel stared with astonishment at the huge sum written in the check's amount box. Suzanne returned carrying a bulging, large mail sack. "Surprise number two." Suzanne upturned the mail sack, spilling out a huge pile of postcards, letters and small parcels of mail. "A shitload of fan mail."

Daniel forced his eyes away from the huge bank check and watched the heap of fan mail now strewn across Suzanne's floor. "Mail for me?" he asked, almost in a little boy's voice. "I've never seen so much... this is amazing." His throat felt tight with emotion. Suzanne momentarily left again, as Daniel surveyed the pile of correspondence with both shock and delight.

Suzanne returned from the other room with two more mail sacks, both larger than the first. She spilled both of them onto the existing pile until the heap of mail on the floor became so thick that the pile rose up almost to their knees. Daniel stood motionless, one hand still holding out the generous check, his eyes wide in shock and his jaw drooping below his neck line, his other hand on his brow.

"You're a sensation," said Suzanne.

"So, all of these people," Daniel said slowly, his brain trying to reason it out, "all of these people actually took the book seriously?"

"Some of them even got results," said Suzanne, thoroughly enjoying the drama of it all.

"What do you mean?"

"Read some of the letters and see for yourself," Suzanne said, taking both of their glasses to the drinks cabinet for refills.

"Mr. John Fox, Tutorsfield, Wisconsin," Daniel read from the envelope as he opened it. "Walking backwards blindfolded while banging two sauce pan lids together and singing *If I Were a Rich Man* at the top of my lungs really helped improve my concentration, as your book said it would. I fell over a couple of times and needed to be treated for a mild concussion and some minor cuts and bruises but the weeklong stay in the hospital was a small price to pay for the heightened awareness which I felt as a result of the exercise. If you're ever in the Wisconsin area..." Daniel stopped reading and looked at Suzanne with a mystified expression.

"Read some more," encouraged Suzanne, handing him his refill.

"How to be a forest fairy, as described in your book, was a hard exercise for me at first. However, as I followed the exercise further and yelled out for all the other forest fairies to come gather round, sure enough, they did reveal themselves from their hiding places and I soon felt myself as one of them. My view of life has changed dramatically as a result." Daniel stopped reading and picked up another letter.

"Dear Charles, I performed the exercise where you read the bible backwards singing the words to the tune of *Happy Birthday to Me* and now, thanks to you, I can hear the voice of Satan telling me to do despicable…"

Suzanne grabbed the letter from his hands. "Yeah, well, not all of them are winners," she said.

"These people are nuts," said Daniel. "We have names and addresses here… we should call the mental health services or something."

"Don't be ridiculous, Daniel," Suzanne said casually. "These are your fans. You've earned quite a following with just one book."

"Yeah, I'm king of the loonies."

"It's the follow-up book that always sells even better."

"What follow-up book?"

"The second in the series," said Suzanne, as if she had a plan already worked out.

"I couldn't write a follow-up," Daniel said, taken aback by the mere suggestion.

"Sure you could. You could sell the telephone book to these people if we gave it a cover with your name on it. It doesn't have to be good or even have any new content. Just do what every other author does when their first book is a surprise hit: repeat everything you said in the first book and pad it out with anecdotes and testimonials."

The way that Daniel looked at Suzanne suggested that maybe for the first time in their relationship he was realizing that he didn't know who she was, either. Is she evil, he wondered or perhaps certifiably insane, just like the rest of humanity?

"Don't you realize what you've tapped into here?" continued Suzanne. "To these people you're a guru... a modern-day prophet. They need you!"

"These people are unbalanced..."

"Who, in their right mind is not unbalanced, Daniel?"

"What?"

"Think about it, Daniel," said Suzanne, searching in her mind for the best mental hook to catch him with. "If they weren't buying your book, they'd be spending their money on crystals and pyramids or something. Why shouldn't you get the money instead of some pot-smoking, New Age charlatans? Why should you starve when you have such a talent for... irony?"

"But that's the point. They don't know that it's irony!"

Suzanne dropped her persuasive intensity and took their glasses back to the cocktail cabinet for replenishment. "I don't know what to think about you, Daniel. You're not stupid but you do seem so incredibly naïve." Suzanne looked back at Daniel to see if he was paying attention. Daniel was staring at the piles of mail, almost transfixed. She wondered what was going through his mind.

"Whether we like it or not, Daniel, writing and selling books is a business," she said, not sure if he was listening or not. "Write something that sells, then you have a career. If not, then you're delivering pizzas. So, the question is: you want to be a writer or a pizza delivery boy?" A full drink in each hand, Suzanne paused for effect. Daniel remained staring at the massive collection of fan mail.

"Look at all this mail!" Daniel finally said, more to himself than as an invite to dialogue.

Suzanne brightened and decided to change tack. "They want you, Daniel," she said, almost seductively. "You have a knowledge that they need. The knowledge of the writer."

Suzanne noticed a slight upturn of Daniel's jaw and sensed that this was the right path of persuasion to pursue. She walked towards him, slowly and deliberately as if not wanting to arouse him from his trance-like state. "You have insight, Daniel. Power. You have the power to move people... to really influence and affect people. Think about that."

"Gee, I don't know," Daniel said weakly, still looking around at all the mail.

"You have a power that even you yourself have yet to fully discover. People around you can feel it. I can feel it." Suzanne moved snake-like, her face was now within inches of Daniel's. "Go with it, Daniel. Explore it for yourself. This book was just for fun. Dig down deep for the second one and let's see what you have buried deep down there. You owe it to these people, Daniel. You owe it to the world." Suzanne grabbed his face and pulled it tighter to hers. "Aren't you even a little curious... about how you could impact people, if you let yourself?"

"I don't know..." Daniel began. Before he could finish his sentence, Suzanne kissed him full on, on the mouth. When they broke off, Daniel looked at her with a mix of astonishment, puzzlement and increasing desire. It has been so long since he had been touched. When she kissed him again, his desire won out over everything else. Their bodies merged in a torrent of uncoiled passion and they drifted to the floor, removing their clothing on the descent, where their intermingling bodies met in a explosion of pent up lust and a feverish need for deep human contact, rollicking and rolling about in a sea of obsequious and devotional fan mail.

SPEND A WEEKEND WITH CHARLES SPECTRUM

"I think I should really explore the human condition in the second one," Daniel said, sitting across from Mavis at their local coffee abode.

"Isn't that what you've been doing in your novels, Daniel?" said Mavis, not buying into his stated and implied altruistic motivation.

"Yes, of course," hedged Daniel. "But this time I mean delving really deep... into what makes us tick, as humans. I haven't written non-fiction before, Mavis. You don't sound terribly supportive."

"I'm sorry, Daniel. *You Have a Brain* is one of the funniest books that I've ever read. I'm just not sure about a sequel."

"But that's just it, Mavis. It doesn't have to be a sequel. I have an audience now... people who will buy whatever it is that I write. It doesn't need to have anything to do with the brain or with improving the mental powers of readers or the like. It is as if I've been handed an opportunity to reach out to common humanity. I've been given a pulpit to speak my mind. I can finally say what I want to say," Daniel said, passionately.

"I see. What is it you want to say, then... to common humanity."

Not wanting to be glib or fail to give due consideration to the enormity of the undertaking at hand, Daniel thought hard about the question for a bit. "I have no idea," he finally answered. "I have absolutely no idea."

For the next few days, aside from taking time out

to trade in his recently-acquired, economically-minded Jetta and pay cash for a brand spanking new, ostentatious Cadillac, and moving to a larger and more opulent condominium, Daniel thought about little else except what his new book would be all about. He'd be writing it under the name of Charles Spectrum and, according to Suzanne and her reference to selling a telephone book, his audience was assured. It seemed easier exploring the human condition through fiction, he realized. Through the feelings and behaviors of his characters, Daniel could shine a light on exactly what it was that makes us human. It seemed easier, in fiction, to reveal how we relate to each other in circumstances that he, as the author, could construct and manipulate for a desired effect.

Writing a non-fiction book was an entirely different proposition, he considered. With non-fiction, the author speaks directly to the reader. Therefore, his customary use of literary devices, symbol, myth and metaphor, were not only not required but would only serve to muddy the waters of the direct author-to-reader communication. It was a conundrum he wished to have solved sooner rather than later, as Suzanne was in constant contact with him, urging him to announce a possible publication date.

He wasn't sure exactly where he stood with Suzanne after their frenzied get together in a sea of fan mail. Although they didn't discuss it the next day, or on any subsequent days thereafter, their relationship to each other certainly shifted. He wasn't quite sure if it was for the better or for the worse. There was something about Suzanne that he had never really felt comfortable with; she exuded a kind of predatory nature that both appalled and attracted him all at the same time. Although he didn't want to think ill of her, and accuse her of using her sexuality to get what it was that she wanted, he didn't want to discount the idea, either.

What a character she'd make for a novel, he thought and smiled to himself.

As for his own behavior that evening? As all his literary predecessors, Hemmingway, Faulkner and Steinbeck et al, would attest, for the author, every experience is grist for the mill; not just the pleasant ones but, perhaps most especially, the sordid and morally ambiguous ones, as well. Grist for the mill, he repeated to himself, suddenly feeling the ghost of Hemmingway descend upon him. Perhaps one day I'll take up boxing, drink whiskey neat and run with the bulls in Pamplona, Spain. Why not, he answered a doubting part of himself; why the hell not? He smiled at the possibilities.

He wondered what Suzanne had thought of the whole guru author nonsense, if indeed, she had thought much of it at all. He had no idea what kind of private life Suzanne led; she had always struck him as the kind of career woman who was married to her job. She had invited him to dinner at her home, which added further complications to Daniel's thought processes. He was sure that, traditionally, when a woman invited a man to her abode for a home-cooked meal that it meant that the woman was interested in the man and wished to pursue their relationship even further. Did he really want to enter into a more personal and intimate relationship with this woman? Just like the confusion that came up for him regarding finding a suitable topic for his new book, he had absolutely no idea.

Daniel arrived at Suzanne's home with the customary gift bottle of wine. He chose not to bring a bouquet of flowers. He didn't wish to appear too presumptuous. Suzanne didn't greet him with a kiss, which Daniel figured would set the tone for the evening. Instead, she opened the front door with both of her hands full; she held a head of lettuce in one hand and a glass of red wine in the other. She wore an apron which had the words: *Just Because I'm The One Wearing an Apron Doesn't Make Me Your Bitch*.

"Come on in," she smiled, quickly examining but not seeming overly impressed with the bottle of wine he held out. "I had to make an unexpected visit to bail my brother out of jail so dinner will be a while," she said, rushing back to the kitchen to check on the contents of a pot on the stove. "Pour yourself a drink," she said, nodding her head towards an open bottle of wine. "How's the new book coming along?" she asked while stirring what looked like some kind of tomato sauce in a large pot.

"It's all that I've been thinking about," answered Daniel, evasively.

"The publishers are very anxious," said Suzanne coolly, still busy cooking.

Daniel smiled and repeated to himself what Suzanne had just said. It has always been his dream, as a writer, to have publishers anxiously awaiting his newest work. Hearing it from Suzanne made him feel that much more important and he noticed that he stood more erect, as a result. "First-rate work can't be rushed, Suzanne," he said, with just a hint of haughtiness.

"They're concerned that demand might get cold by the time that the book *does* get written and finally goes to print. It could take up to a year to get it onto the shelves. This kind of readership is fickle, Daniel. Until you build up some brand loyalty, they'll jump onto the next, newest fad that comes along." Suzanne checked the foods simmering on the stove.

"It's my top priority, Suzanne, trust me." She looked at him skeptically.

"We need to keep the interest level high and maintain your presence and visibility in the market place." Suzanne turned off the stove, mixed the pasta and sauce in a bowl, and motioned for Daniel to follow her into the dining room.

"Sure," said Daniel, agreeing to something he didn't totally understand.

"This is a mock-up of the new brochure," she said, handing him a colorful brochure; his picture and an image of the book, front and center.

"What's this?" asked Daniel, casually. As he read it further, some alarm bells began to ring in his brain. "Seminars?"

"*Use Your Brain*... the seminar. Spend a weekend with Charles Spectrum, expanding your brain power and becoming a better human. You could be the new Randy Guswhite," Suzanne said excitedly.

"I don't want to be the new... anybody. I don't want to be doing seminars, Suzanne," Daniel said in a derogatory tone. "I'm a writer... a man-of-letters. I extend influence and reach my audience through the written word."

"Daniel Waterstone is a failed man of letters, Daniel. Charles Spectrum is a successful motivational writer... an emerging spiritual guide. Come... sit. Let's eat." Suzanne quickly placed pots and plates of food on the dining table.

Daniel sat at the table and could barely hold in his contempt for what Suzanne was suggesting he become. She stared at him. He glared back. Her eyes narrowed.

"You haven't even started on the new book, have you?" asked Suzanne.

"No...I—"

"You don't even know what you're going to write about, do you?"

"Not exactly. I've made progress... some notes..."

"Don't you understand?" Suzanne said intently, "By the time you get your act together and hand something in, the publishers have already forgotten about you and guess, what? After all the thought and the research and the planning; after all the work you've just gone through, they reject your novel. It's too this, it's too that... sound familiar? You know what that feels like, right? Some salad?" Suzanne held out the salad bowl for Daniel who took a few seconds to react and add some of the greens and tomato to his plate. Then he helped himself to some of the pasta dish. Seeing that Suzanne was about to launch into another diatribe, Daniel knocked back the rest of his glass of wine. He was grateful that Suzanne immediately filled it.

"Speaking of Randy Guswhite," Suzanne continued, speaking between bites of food. "The guy has gone AWOL. He's cancelled his speaking engagements, pulled his Twitter, Facebook and web sites and, no surprise, his book just collapsed... fell right down the charts, out of sight. Went from being a top ten best seller to a nothing, in pretty much the blink of an eye. I don't make the rules, Daniel; it's an instant gratification, attention deficit disorder book-buying public out there. He puts out another book, he'll have to start from scratch, all over again. Have some more wine."

Daniel helped himself to another very large glass of Suzanne's finest.

"We'll promote and hold some speaking engagements so that readers can get to meet the author. Not only will you keep your existing readers but these kind of events also help to extend your fan base. So, when the second book finally gets printed, pre-order sales ensure that it hits the ground running and makes the best-seller lists right out the gate. It's perfect. You don't like the Chicken Parmesan?" He looked down at the food on his plate adjacent to his salad; it was chicken with cheese and tomato sauce on top of pasta.

"Oh, no, I mean, yeah. It's all very good, thank you," said Daniel. Flustered, he couldn't admit that, despite the delicious-looking home-cooked meal, he had completely lost his appetite.

"Think of it as doing a book tour, Daniel. You had a

little taste of that with your first book, right?" said Suzanne, referring to the scant few book store signings and public library discussions which Daniel had attended when he was starting out.

"These readers love you, Daniel. All you have to do is just show up and they're going to fawn all over you. What's the worst that can happen? You get loved to death?"

"If I don't know what to write, how am I going to know what to say?"

"You read from the brain book. Open it up to questions. If they believe everything you write, they're going to believe everything that you say. You're Moses to these people. Lead them to the promised land," Suzanne said in teasing tone, hoping to brighten his mood.

"Oh, right. The people need a leader. I don't think so."

"I saw your expression when my assistant Sidney told you that you changed his life. That was a really good feeling, right? When someone reads your book and says that to you?"

"I guess."

"Multiply that by thousands, Daniel. What kind of a feeling would that be, huh? Think about it."

A warm feeling gushed through Daniel's body as he thought about what it would feel like to have thousands of people tell him that his writing had changed their lives for the better. As Suzanne refilled both their glasses of wine, Daniel visibly jumped in his chair when a short, stocky man walked through the dining room doorway. He was either naturally bald or a shaved skinhead, it was hard to tell. He had scary-looking, prison-like tattoos all over his body. He wore a bath towel around his waist, as if he just stepped out of the shower.

"Where do you keep the blankets, Suzi?" he said, without any acknowledgement of Daniel.

"The cupboard right beside the bathroom, egghead," Suzanne said with intimate familiarity. "Jack, this is Charles Spectrum, the man you're going to be working for."

"Yo," said Jack.

"Yo," Daniel automatically repeated back to him.

"If there's anything else it can wait till tomorrow. We're kinda in a meeting here," Suzanne said, perhaps acknowledging that Jack looked like he was in no hurry to return to wherever it was that he had come from. "I'll leave you some leftovers, okay?"

"Sweet," replied Jack, still looking like something was on his mind. She shrugged her shoulders as if to say, what's up. "You're running low on booze," he finally stated.

"I'll pick some up tomorrow, sweetie," Suzanne said, with an air of finality.

"Okay," Jack said with a tinge of disappointment. "That'll work."

When Jack departed the room, Suzanne continued eating but didn't comment.

"Who's Jack?" Daniel asked, curious out of his mind.

"Jack's my little brother. I'll be looking after him for a while. He's the black sheep of the family." Suzanne tossed back the rest of her glass of wine.

"What do you mean, you're looking after him?" Daniel said, eyebrows raised.

"I'm his indemnitor. I put up the bail money."

"What did he..." Thinking that maybe it was way too personal, Daniel didn't finish the question and instead took a bite of food and chewed rapidly.

"Like I say. He's the black sheep," said Suzanne with a weariness that suggested a long history of sibling travails.

"And he's going to be working for me?" Daniel asked, frightened but trying to sound neutral.

"I'm going to have him work security," Suzanne said,

calmly. "It'll give him something to do and I can keep an eye on him."

"Sure," said Daniel, perplexed but wanting to sound agreeable. "Security for what?"

"No more questions about my brother, Daniel, if you don't mind," said Suzanne, already exhausted by the conversation. "What you need to focus on is what you're going to be saying to your multitude of fans."

"Multitude?" repeated Daniel, more of a statement than as a question.

THE MULTITUDE OF FANS

Daniel nervously peaked out at the arriving fans, who were casually taking their seats, in a large banquet room at the Vacation Inn and Suites near downtown Los Angeles. Despite the fact that they looked like a normal cross-section of society (arty types, business people, dating couples, married couples, assorted single persons) and a broad mix of age groups, Daniel was still petrified.

"There you are," said Suzanne with obvious relief upon discovering Daniel. "We thought you had bailed on us. It's natural to be nervous, you know. You wouldn't be human if you weren't."

"I'm not nervous, Suzanne. I'm terrified."

"Here, let me put this on you," said Suzanne as she placed a heavy red colored robe or "cape thing" around Daniel's shoulders.

"What's this?" asked Daniel, looking the thing up and down with immeasurable contempt.

"These are your power robes," Suzanne said casually. "Speakers like to wear them the same way actors like to wear a costume. They don't feel so naked going out on stage in front of a live audience."

"I can't go out looking like this," argued Daniel, "I look like a crazy person."

"You look exactly like what someone like Charles Spectrum would look like, Daniel: mysterious, powerful and different than the rest of us. A man of mystery, you have secrets that no one else possesses…"

"Oh, give me a break," interjected Daniel. "I'm a joke of an author walking out on stage in the Vacation Inn draped in a goofy-looking robe made from left-over red velvet curtains. This is a complete farce and they're going to boo me off stage or, worse, hang me from the cheap plastic chandelier and then ask for their money back. I agreed to a bookstore signing, that's all."

"Daniel, in case you haven't noticed, all of the book stores have gone out of business. We've got a table at the back for you to sign autographs, after you go out there and say a few words. You're an author doing a book signing in the Vacation Inn. What's the big deal?"

"The big deal is I don't like people," said Daniel, surprising himself with his honesty. "I especially don't like it when they get together in groups. They remind me of pack animals."

"Just take a few deep breaths, say a few words and all this will be over before you know it. Trust me, you'll knock 'em dead." Suzanne was already tired of his hang-up.

"Yeah, right," said Daniel, unconvinced and still very, very afraid.

"Listen to me," Suzanne said, grabbing his shoulders and looking him in the eyes. "Just talk to them as if you were talking to a good friend. Give them the benefit of your experience; share your innermost thoughts and be truthful and honest. Don't belittle them or speak down to them. Tell them all the stuff that you wrote in your book; tell them that it's okay to feel alone; it hurts to feel alone and that you know and understand their pain; you can feel their pain... You wrote such brilliant stuff, Daniel. Go share it with the world."

Daniel looked at Suzanne with incredible unease. Although her words did indeed strengthen and fortify him for his forthcoming ordeal, the fact that the words were coming from her mouth... he just couldn't deduce whether she was speaking from her heart—which is what it sounded like—or some other place of pretense from within her. Perhaps she was saying the words, with the required gravitas, but inwardly was laughing her friggin' head off.

Before he gained clarity about the intention behind Suzanne's words, she was pushing him toward the curtain and the stage.

"Ladies and gentlemen, give a rousing and warm reception for... Mr. Charles Spectrum!" was heard over the PA system.

"Go to your people, Daniel. They're going to love you," said Suzanne with no telltale smirk on her face.

Daniel took some final deep breaths and walked out onto the stage just as the polite applause faded. As soon as he made eye contact with the audience, in terror, his feet immediately stopped walking.

Time seemed to slow for Daniel. He stood motionless, surveying the well attended event. The lights looked blurry; indeed his entire vision seemed out of focus, the scene before him seeming dreamlike and distorted. His experience of external audio also seemed to have slowed down, so that, acoustically, everything sounded as if he were listening underwater.

It wasn't until he realized that, one by one, each of the assembled members of the audience had gotten to their feet, their arms swinging wildly in a rousing applause, that his vision and hearing began to correct and come into real time. His brain then interpreted the scene before him: he had received a standing ovation for simply walking out on stage.

Taking in the waves of warmth and appreciation emanating from the broadly smiling audience before him, Daniel became more energized and alive. An unconscious large smile broke out upon his face and his feet took him slowly forward. "Hello," he said with magisterial authority, "my name... is Charles Spectrum."

As the applause continued, and grew even louder, Daniel felt the spirit rise up within him and quickly grow and expand to equal the measure of their euphoric encouragement. As the growing applause reached a deafening and rapturous crescendo, Daniel's arms rose aloft in a triumphant display of victorious approval. It was as if he was Caesar himself, greeting the citizens of Rome after a successful conquest of the neighboring hordes of rebellious pagan barbarians.

"Charles Spectrum is in the house," a relieved and now smirking Suzanne said, in a snarky aside, to her assistant, Sidney.

"Isn't he just glorious?" Sidney said in reverential awe and completely missing her smugly-coated sarcasm.

"Glorious, indeed, Sidney. Glorious indeed," Suzanne said, more to herself than anyone else.

As the applause finally died down and people began sitting back in their seats, Daniel surveyed the room with deliberate cognizance; never before experiencing such enthusiastic adulation in his life, his self-assurance and overall confidence level was through the roof.

"By deciding to attend this seminar, each one of you has embarked upon a mission... a mission to acquire more self-knowledge and greater self-understanding; to... "know thyself," to use the ancient maxim of Plato and the Temple of Apollo at Delphi. Now, some of you may eventually find that such an acquisition wasn't worth the effort, after all... but that's okay," said Daniel with a smile which got broader as the audience broke into a spontaneous laugh. Surprising himself, Daniel had not known before that he could be so off-the-cuff funny.

Unseen, from behind a screen at the side of the makeshift stage, Suzanne scanned the faces of the audience, trying to gauge their interest levels. Smiling, she liked what she saw: intent facial expressions; people sitting upright in their seats; people writing in notebooks; heads craned forward, rapt listeners hoping not to miss a single word uttered. "Way to go, Dan," she said, under her breath.

"What's going on?" asked her brother Jack, as he appeared at her side.

"You're late," said Suzanne, turning to face him with a stern expression. Her face tightened further when she saw what he was wearing: camouflage cargo pants and jacket with a peaked cap. "What are you wearing?" she asked with puzzled bewilderment. Thinking that there was absolutely nothing wrong with his attire, Jack checked himself out and wasn't sure what kind of a response he was expected to give. "Don't you have a suit?" Suzanne asked pointedly.

"A suit?" replied Jack, like it was a crazy question.

"What do you think this is? Militia boot camp? This is a professional job; you need to look like a professional. Go buy yourself a suit," said Suzanne raiding her own purse and holding out a credit card.

"You don't always have to perform the disapproving big sister act, you know," said Jack, looking somewhat humiliated and hurt.

"Who said I disapprove?" Suzanne said, her tone instantly softened. "This is a potentially big thing for me and I want it to go smoothly, that's all. I guess I'm a bit nervous," she said, not seeming one bit nervous. "You're going to look terrific in a suit. What do you think?"

"I guess," answered Jack, his head bowed he retreated toward the exit.

"Hurry back!" Suzanne sweetly called after him. She waved and hoped that he saw her smile. As Jack vanished through the exit door, Suzanne returned her attention to Daniel's presentation. Looking more relaxed and self-assured than she'd ever seen him, he commanded the stage with an impressive sense of authority that actually turned her on a bit.

"Somewhere in our evolution we became conscious of ourselves, which, it turns out, is something of a mixed blessing. Why? Well, I'm aware of myself as an individual... which is good, right? But being self aware, I realize that I'm alone. I'm so aware of myself that I feel cut off from everything and everyone else. I'm alone with my thoughts; these incessant thoughts that keep asking all of these unanswerable questions like, who am I? Right? I have self-consciousness; I'm self-aware... but who am I? Who is this person that I think I am that thinks he is self-aware, is aware of himself, and aware that he is alone?"

The audience was so totally there with Daniel that Suzanne smiled broadly. Her expression said that this was going better than she ever had hoped that it would.

"Who am I?" said Daniel, pausing for dramatic emphasis. The audience stared and held their collective bated breath, and waited for him to continue.

"No matter whether you are aware of it or not, this one solitary question informs every thought that you think, every act that you take and every plan which you make for the future. Why? Because the question is so basic, so fundamental to your identity, to your core self, to who you define yourself as being, that it's paramount that you know the answer. But guess what? You don't have an answer, do you? Who are you?" Daniel scanned the attentive faces of the audience, as if waiting for someone to answer his question. No one budged.

"You don't have the answer, do you? Oh, sure, you can say, "I'm me," but that's not an answer, is it? Who is "me?" And who is the "me" that's asking "me" the question? Are there two of me?" Daniel again paused; perhaps he himself was not sure where he was going with his argument. Daniel waited a long moment and appeared lost in thought. The audience was mesmerized and sat in complete unmoving silence.

"Because we cannot successfully answer this very basic question about ourselves - whether we're aware of it or not - the *not* knowing causes us great anxiety. How can we be anything or do anything or think anything when we don't even know who we are? Not only do I not know who I am but to compound my internal distress, why am I so terribly alone?

A number of attendees, deeply moved by the direction that the lecture had gone, silently wept. Others sat and paid rapt attention to Daniel's every word. Still others wrote down every word that he said. There were no inattentive people in attendance.

"Ladies and gentlemen, we could debate which gruesome torture that man has invented is the worst; is it water-boarding or sleep deprivation while being forced to listen to heavy metal rock music? Rather than waste time discussing that, let me tell you that the most cruel and unusual punishment known to man is not a method of torture that we inflict upon each other; the worst and absolute deadly and most insidious form of torture already afflicts each and every one of us constantly. It is non-stop and incessant. Like a broken record, playing in the deep, dark recesses of our brains, repeating in an endless loop just below the threshold of conscious awareness, playing over and over, are those two fundamental and ultimately unanswerable questions: 'Who am I?' and 'Why am I so terribly, terribly alone?'"

Daniel paused to take some deep breaths and possibly to gather his thoughts further. The audience sat in silent rapture, many nodding their heads in agreement.

"And because we can't answer these questions," Daniel began once more, "they continue to repeat, over and over and over again. But because we don't know the answers, we block out the questions; we hold our metaphorical hands to our metaphorical ears and we sing a song, or make enough noise, to drown out the constant badgering, just the way a parent might react to a child that kept repeating the question: 'Why? Why? Why? Why? Why? Why?'

"We may have blocked out the questioning, yet that doesn't really resolve anything, does it? It merely buys us time. We get on with our lives and make something of ourselves, right? We distract ourselves with entertainment. We pursue successful relationships. Well, guess what? No matter what kind of life you make for yourself; no matter how successful you may become in your career or in your private life, these fundamental questions continue to go unaddressed and as long as they go unanswered... how does it make you feel?"

The facial expressions of the audience suggested that they were deep in thought, trying perhaps to answer the question that Daniel had proposed.

"I'll tell you how that makes you feel: like a fraud." As Daniel answered his own question, many in the audience shifted uneasily in their seats. "Sure, you've got a nice home, a nice car and money in the bank and a loving spouse and healthy kids but you still feel like a fraud, right? You feel like a fraud because you have no idea of the who it is that has the nice home and the career and the loving spouse and all the rest of it."

"Or maybe you don't have nice things. Possibly you're struggling to get by, to pay your bills... and you've never had a meaningful personal or professional relationship. Perhaps you don't have friends or your health." More audience members wept silently.

"You still feel the same, though. You still feel like a fraud," Daniel said with conviction.

Suzanne watched the assembled listen intently. She was entirely nonplussed by the people, in the minority, who were extremely emotional as the bulk of the audience paid rapt attention to Daniel's every word. Terribly excited by the dynamics of Daniel's seminar, Suzanne happily texted her troops to alert them to prepare for the forthcoming stages of her successful "Charles Spectrum" roll out strategy. It would occupy their, and her, every moment in the days and weeks to come.

"I'm a fraud," announced Daniel, from the midst of his seemingly smooth and unstoppable performance. Several members of the audience gasped. "And you're a fraud... and you're a fraud... and you're a fraud..." he said and pointed to the audience, in general.

"We're all frauds. And just as all the twelve-step programs teach us, as soon as we can admit the truth to ourselves, then we can address our fundamental issues and step onto the path to healing, to greater integration, to the road home, wherever that may lead us. I hope you all stick around and we can explore where that might lead us the next time. Thank you."

A few moments of absolute silence passed before, in dribs and drabs, the members of the audience began to applaud and then rose to their feet in an enthusiastic display of respect and appreciation. It went on for some time. Each time that Daniel tried to leave the stage he was forced to return. The audience just did not want to let him go.

Daniel bowed and then exited the stage and entered a side room where Suzanne awaited him. Like an actor having just performed in some emotional high-stakes

Shakespearian play all evening, Daniel was on a high and seemed to be in an other-worldly frame of mind.

"That was fantastic, Daniel," beamed Suzanne, helping him out of his "power" robes. "You were amazing."

"I was, wasn't I?" answered Daniel, who seemed more surprised than anybody. "I have no idea if any of that even makes any sense," he said, as if questioning his entire presentation. "I've no idea where any of that came from," he said with obvious befuddlement. "I guess I just told them what they wanted to hear, right? All that stuff in the brain book?"

"You know you're not done, yet," said Suzanne, checking her watch. "You still have to sign their books at the table set up at the back, okay? An average of two minutes chat with each person... should be out of here within two hours. This is the easy part of the evening."

"Yeah," answered Daniel, absent-mindedly, his brain still replaying his impromptu speech, as if trying to make sense of it all. "Have you ever considered, Suzanne," he asked, thoughtfully, "whether or not there are parts to us... different personalities, perhaps... within us, which we ourselves have yet to become aware of?"

"You know what?" replied Suzanne, quickly. "That's such a wonderful topic to explore for your next talk! You should write all that stuff down and make some notes. What do you think?"

"Yeah, I think maybe... it could be something to explore, right? It's not too... abstract?"

"Nothing's too abstract for these people, Daniel. Abstract is what they live for. Are you good to go?" Suzanne asked hurriedly and looked at her watch.

"Yeah," answered Daniel, as if he was actually looking forward to rejoining the fray. "I'm good to go." Daniel revisited the main room and was welcomed warmly by the mostly full crowd who had been waiting patiently for his return. They applauded him with cheers and broad smiles as he made his way to the book-signing table.

One by one they filed past him, their well-worn copies of the brain book clutched tightly in their hands, eager for his signature. While writing his very first autograph, as Charles Spectrum, Daniel made an error and wrote a large D. Then he caught himself and wrote *Don't be afraid to question* and then signed it, Charles Spectrum. Each time he signed his pseudonym, it was as if he was using the opportunity to develop his signature style. He played around with writing a small C for Charles and then writing an equally small S for Spectrum. He started with the letters going straight, then slanted forward, until finally, after many such signatures, he settled for larger capitals and the writing slanted forwards, finishing it off with a grand flourish, underlining the name with a double curlicue.

As the last of his admiring fans left looking happier and feeling better about themselves than when they entered, Clare uneasily approached his table with a copy of his book for signing.

"That was wonderful, Charles," she beamed, "really wonderful."

"Thank you," said Daniel, feeling awkward and failing to remember her name. "How have you been?"

"Good, thank you," Clare responded, "very good."

"That's good," echoed Daniel, signing her book. "That's really good."

"You, uh... you never got back to me... like you said you would," said Clare with obvious embarrassment. "I was just wondering if it was something I said or..." She didn't finish the sentence, hoping perhaps that he would have interjected sooner.

"Oh, no, not at all. Things have been so busy..." said

Daniel, trying unsuccessfully to sound genuine. "We should... I should... let me check my calendar." Daniel turned and bent down and fumbled through his briefcase, searching for his day planner. Taking it out, he turned back around, and opened it, as if to schedule some kind of meeting. He was just about to speak when he saw her exiting the room with great speed and humiliation. "Shit," he said to himself. It was the first time in the whole evening where he actually felt like a phony.

His lack of honesty coupled with the look of humiliation on the pretty girl's face as she practically ran from the banquet room, left a bad taste in Daniel's conscience and bothered him for the rest of the evening. As he reflexively accepted an invitation for a celebratory nightcap back at Suzanne's place, his earlier mood of triumph and exhilaration was slowly replaced by a more familiar inner state of mental questioning and self-doubt. The more that Suzanne talked excitedly about future plans, the grumpier and grumpier that he became.

"Projected figures should double with the new book and are expected to triple with strategically-placed press coverage," Suzanne said with unabashed enthusiasm as she poured them both some double brandies. "It's not just going to be a local operation anymore, Daniel; we're going nationwide by the end of the month..."

Noticing Daniel's gloomy mood for the first time, Suzanne reluctantly stopped her train of thought in order to check in with Daniel's latest variegated mood state. "What's up?" she asked, repressing her urge to slap him hard. "You don't seem as excited as I expected you would?"

"Why is it that every time we get together..." Daniel started, not really knowing what it was that was bothering him. "It's like, all you talk about is... business speak."

"I'm your agent, Daniel. What do you expect me to be

talking about? I'm discussing our plans for the new book."

"I'm not writing a new book!" Daniel said, his sudden defiance surprising even himself.

"Then get started!" Suzanne said with equal rebelliousness. When she saw Daniel's lips purse and tighten, she very reluctantly realized that she would have to curtail her anger and transform to a softer emotional stance in order to shift his mood and resolve. She inwardly resented having to do such a thing, yet accepted that business was business.

"With the new book we can go big on marketing, advance sales, merchandising tie-ins..." Suzanne said, making it sound as seductive as she possibly could.

Jack abruptly entered, wearing his new, ill-fitted suit. "What do you think?" he asked Suzanne, not even caring if he was rudely interrupting.

"You bought off the rack?" Suzanne asked derisively. "You can't buy a suit off the rack... Look at you! You need to get fitted for a suit."

"I tried it on in the store and the guy said it was perfect," Jack said defensively. "I never wanted it anyway. If it looks like crap, I'll just go back to..."

"It's fine," Suzanne interrupted. "Just maybe the sleeves could be a tad longer but you know what? You look fabulous. Doesn't he look fabulous, Daniel?"

"I wouldn't go so far as to say..." said Daniel before he was given a daggers look by Suzanne. "It's a really nice suit," Daniel corrected himself, without telling a lie.

"I can't find my aftershave lotion," Jack pondered out loud.

"It stank, Jack. I threw it out," answered Suzanne. "I'll get you something a little less... intense, okay?"

"You threw it out?" asked Jack, mystified as to why anyone would throw out an almost full and perfectly good aftershave lotion that wasn't totally the cheapest brand on the store shelf.

"Jack, we're kind of in a meeting."

"Okay," said Jack, somewhat petulantly. "Just don't touch my stuff again, yeah?" he said as a parting admonition and left the room. "We're not in high school anymore."

"And what do I need a bodyguard for, exactly?" asked Daniel.

"It's precautionary. You're becoming a best-selling, celebrity author, Daniel. We can't afford for anything to happen to you right now, can we?"

"Suzanne, I'm a writer, not a rock star."

"It's a crazy world out there, Daniel, full of crazy people. Trust me. I read your fan mail." Suzanne dimmed the lights and put on some soft music. "Anyway, you're right. Enough business speak for the night," she said, shifting into sex kitten mode. "Can I fix you another brandy or do you want to switch to that nice wine that you like so much? There's a glass or two left in the open bottle."

"You know what, Suzanne?" Daniel said with a resolve that sounded like it couldn't easily be broken. "It's been a crazy, hectic day. If you don't mind, I'd like to head off before I drink too much to drive home. Maybe then I'll get a good night's rest and start working on that new book first thing tomorrow. Rain check?"

"Sure," said Suzanne, sounding unsure but equally uncertain about what her next move should be. "Get some good rest and get into that new book. Glad to hear the plan."

"Ciao," waved Daniel cheerfully as he opened the door, hoping she wouldn't approach him for a hug or a kiss or any other suggestion of impending or past intimate involvement.

"Ciao," repeated Suzanne, to her now empty room. She gazed at the glass of amber brandy in hand, then decided to down it in one serious gulp.

THE RETURN OF RANDY GUSWHITE

Randy Guswhite sat at the counter in a dark, non-descript dive bar anonymously located on a side street off of Hollywood Boulevard. He looked more like a permanent fixture, the kind of man who sat in the same spot every day, rather than someone who had just popped in for a quick one on the way home from working hard all day. Beside him sat a stranger, looking equally at home in the bar which he probably referred to as his second home. Depressed and overweight, the stranger kept checking out Randy's reflection in the mirror, as if he maybe knew him from someplace but wasn't quite sure where.

"Don't I know you from somewhere?" the depressed, overweight man eventually said to Randy.

Randy took a good hard look at the stranger. "Who are you?" he asked.

"Freddie West," said the man, extending his hand. "I'm a journalist."

Randy didn't shake Freddie's hand but instead closed his eyes in what looked like painful concentration. "You work for the Times," Randy said, expecting positive confirmation.

"I don't work for the *Times*, no," said Freddie.

Shaking his head as self-admonishment for being incorrect, Randy quickly placed his massive right hand on Freddie's head. Instantly freaked, Freddie jerked his head back.

"Keep your hands to yourself, man," he said, wondering to himself if the guy was dangerous.

"You're a journalist for the *Globe*!" Randy exclaimed,

118

quite obviously again expecting his intuition to be correct.

"No, I used to work for *The Inquiry*," said Freddie, then added almost apologetically, "until I got writer's block."

"I know exactly how you feel," commiserated Randy. "I've got mental block."

"A 'mental' block?" asked Freddie, something he has never heard of.

"I lost my powers," confided Randy. "I can't read minds anymore, obviously," he said pointedly, and shrugged to indicate his obvious exceedingly recent failure to intuit Freddie's employer.

Freddie suddenly brightened up, now recognizing his drinking buddy. "You're that guy... that motivational guy with the crazy mind powers... Randy Guswhite!" Freddie expected more from Randy than a non-reactive, cold stare, as if Randy was looking right past him. "What?" asked Freddie, a little alarmed. "What are you staring at?"

"It's him!" Randy exclaimed and shot off of his bar stool to grab a newspaper out of the hands of a small business-looking gent. The man was in the midst of reading and quite shocked to have his paper ripped from his hands.

"Hey!" shouted the gent but then instantly changed his tune when he saw exactly how large the newspaper thief was. "You can borrow it, no problem," he said weakly.

Meanwhile, Randy was raging over some newspaper article which made Freddie wildly curious to know what it was. "What is it? What is it?" he asked excitedly, trying to follow Randy's eyes to the article in question.

"The mind meld!" Randy declared, as if finally putting the pieces together in a way that allowed him to solve a perplexing puzzle. "He really did steal my brain," he said, pointing to Daniel's photo which adorned a large advertisement for Charles Spectrum's best-selling brain book.

"Steal your what, now?" asked Freddie, looking at the advertisement for clues.

"Him!" said Randy, slapping the newspaper with his finger tips. "He's a fraud! He stole my mind!"

"He stole your mind?" asked Freddie, wondering if he could possibly have heard the man right.

"I have to get it back!" extorted Randy, his wild thoughts propelling and almost preparing him to take action. He looked at Freddie, his eyes bulging from his sweaty and increasingly red face. "That man must be stopped. He's a thief and a fraud!" Randy grabbed his jacket, threw some bills down on the counter for his tab and swiftly walked to the bar exit.

Freddie quickly scanned the advertisement, his mind excitedly making connections and working out the broad outlines of a possible story; a rough headline already appearing on the *Inquiry* front page in his mind's eye: *STOP THIEF! FRAUD STEALS RANDY GUSWHITE'S BRAIN*. What the hell, he thought to himself as he absent-mindedly grabbed his coat; as crazy as it sounds, it's a story that just fell into my lap. Might as well follow it up and see where it takes me.

"Hey!" the business gent half-heartedly exclaimed as Freddie left the bar with the article. "That's my newspaper!"

§

Daniel stepped out before a large, adoring crowd in the main auditorium of the Hollywood Playhouse, which was almost full to capacity. Dressed in his power robes and exuding authority and confidence, his arms extended in a welcoming gesture, he walked to the very brink of the stage as if to get to the possible closest point between the audience and himself. Basking in their loud and rapturous standing ovation, he made no attempt to quell their fervor or in any way tone down their appreciative applause. He merely waited for their expression of adoration to evolve into a respectful silence.

"My name is Charles Spectrum," he said, as the applause began to fade. As if he had just stoked their fires of admiration with his benign declaration, the audience quickly stood again and passionately applauded some more. This time, he did flourish his arms downwards to signal his grateful, yet humble appreciation. The room grew hushed.

"I know that most, if not all of you, have many questions to ask and many of you have come here looking for answers; answers that perhaps you can't find anywhere else." Daniel paused, taking in the grand assemblage, each of them attentive, many of them shaking their heads in acknowledgment and agreement. "I'm here to tell you that, if indeed that is the case, then you are in for a very disappointing evening." The audience became even more attentive; some whispered words of shared concern to each other; some people adjusted themselves uneasily in their seats. Other audience members gaped at Daniel.

"Let me be the first person to admit it to you... I do not have the answers to the questions that you so desperately seek."

Suzanne stood in the wings, watching the reactions of the audience and listening just as attentively to Daniel as they were. Perhaps she too, was wondering where he was going with this line of thought.

"You may be surprised to know, and perhaps some of you may even be astounded to discover, that you didn't even have to get in your cars and drive to attend here this evening. You all could have all stayed at home." As Daniel continued, Suzanne was now visibly squirming in her seat, almost as much as most of the audience was in theirs.

Where was he going with this?

"But then, we wouldn't learn anything, we wouldn't find out the answers to our very many questions, I hear you say. Well, guess what? The answers that you so rabidly seek are not to be found wheresoever's you look. Would you be amazed to discover that you already knew the answers to your questions... all along? That the answers to your questions were within your reach, yet you didn't even notice?"

Daniel paused and walked pensively to the other side of the stage.

"Have you ever looked all over for your eye glasses only to have someone eventually point to the top of your head, which is where you secured them at some moment when you didn't immediately need them?" Daniel stared into the audience; many of them were now smiling and nodding their heads in recognition. Suzanne sighed with relief.

"Have you ever looked everywhere for the pencil that you were just using to do the crossword puzzle but couldn't find it until someone pointed out to you that it was wedged above your ear, all along?" Again Daniel paused as smiles of identification appeared on attendees faces and little chuckles over such moments rippled among the attendees.

"If this has happened to you, or something very similar, then you know what it feels like to have something like that pointed out to you, right? Did you feel foolish?"

Many in the audience smiled and responded in the affirmative.

"Did you feel a sense of relief? Ah, that's where it was! I've been looking all over the place for that! I never would I have found it until someone pointed it out to me. You know?"

Along with the rest of the audience, Suzanne smiled

and sat back in her chair.

"Consider that the answers to your questions are right there... but because you're looking everywhere else than where they actually are... so you're not going to find them. Perhaps you may need someone to point them out to you. Let's try an exercise."

Enjoying the show, the audience shuffled about in their seats in excited expectation.

"I want you to pair up with the person next to you, on your right. Doesn't matter if you know them or not, they are going to be your outside pair of eyes for this one exercise. I want you all to stand up, quickly introduce yourselves and face each other."

The entire crowd rose to their feet and paired up with enthusiasm. Clare Peterson, who looked to be enjoying the talk, paired up with an older gentleman, who clearly appreciated his good fortune as he smiled to her and nodded a "hello."

"I want you to think of a question that you would dearly love to know the answer to. And I don't mean who is going to win the World Series... you know the kind of abstract question I'm talking about." Many of the audience laughed, which helped to settle any nervousness that they may have been feeling as they faced off, in most cases, with an absolute stranger.

"Imagine that the answer is that pair of glasses, propped upon the head of the person opposite you. Why don't you join the palms of your hands to your partner's palms, so that you're not so far apart from each other. It may also help to close your eyes so as to enhance your concentration. Don't allow yourself to become distracted by what's going on with everyone else."

As the audience cooperatively complied, Randy Guswhite entered the theatre foyer from the street. Looking agitated, he carried a copy of the *You Have a Brain!* book and scoffed loudly at a giant-sized cut-out of Daniel, as Charles Spectrum, many of which adorned various areas of the entrance and foyer, along with the caption, *An Evening With Charles Spectrum and your Brain*.

He pulled the handle to the door of the main entrance but, as it was locked, it didn't budge. Undeterred, he made his way to the side entrance on his right. Soon discovering that it too was locked, he looked through a glass panel in the door. From where he was standing, he saw that the entire audience was on their feet and matched up in what looked like to him as a variation of the mind meld exercise.

"I knew it!" he exclaimed out loud, all his assertions and fears of out-and-out theft and fraud, completely vindicated. Once again he tried the door, rattling it hard but it still remained closed. Sidney, acting as an usher, popped up at the other side of the door and peered out at Randy with an inquisitive look.

"Let me in! Do you hear me? He's a fraud," shouted Randy, although to Sidney's ears, all he could hear was muffled, incoherent ramblings. "He's a fraud and he must be stopped!" shouted Randy. Sidney signaled to Randy that he couldn't allow entry. As Randy continued to shout and gesture wildly with his giant arms, Sidney grew concerned and spoke into his walkie-talkie, calling for front-of-house assistance.

"What's the problem, man?" Jack said as he approached a still, very agitated Randy.

"I need to get in," Randy replied, after he consciously calmed himself down, purposefully slowing his breathing, so as not to seem like a crazy person.

"They close the doors, once the seminar begins," explained Jack. "If you keep your ticket, they might let you take the next one." He looked Randy up and down. Randy nodded.

"That sounds good to me," agreed Randy, choosing compliance over aggravation. "Thank you. I'll do that," he said as he walked off. Jack stared after him.

At the conclusion of the presentation, the attendees streamed out of the auditorium, all looking very happy and uplifted. Some of them had obviously been weeping. Others almost glowed, with a beatific light, of sorts.

Daniel packed away his stuff and couldn't help but feel a bit crowded by Jack, who stood right before him, arms folded and steely-eyed, Daniel's personal "security watchdog" who gazed at the last few remaining people who moved slowly from the auditorium.

As Daniel walked away, he quickly remembered that he left his pen behind. Turning quickly to go and retrieve it, he bumped right into Jack who had been following behind, tight on his heel.

"Do you really think this security thing is necessary?" asked Daniel, feeling very smothered.

"Just doing my job," replied Jack, rather stoically. From his attitude, it could be interpreted that he didn't seem to think much of Daniel or his security gig.

Daniel left the auditorium and headed for the men's room. Jack followed. "Why don't you stay outside and stand guard here, okay?" said Daniel with obvious impatience. "If I need you, I'll call. How's that?"

"Don't be long," replied Jack, evidently unsure about the impromptu arrangement.

"I won't even wash my hands," Daniel said with obvious sarcasm. Jack didn't get the joke.

Daniel selected an empty stall, pulled his pants down, and sat on the toilet. He rubbed his forehead and sighed and then casually took a look at the tabloid newspaper which was draped around the handicapped rail. He smirked to himself when he discovered that it was a copy of the *National Inquiry* whose front page headline read, MY HUSBAND IS AN ALIEN.

As his eyes casually flitted from headline to what seemed like an even crazier headline, a giant pair of hands descended down towards Daniel's unsuspecting head. Seeing a shadow move across the newspaper, Daniel casually turned his head to glance up. What he saw sent his heart racing: Randy Guswhite was reaching over the stall partition with his arms outstretched towards Daniel's head.

"I don't want to hurt you," Randy said quietly and his voice wavered in an almost demented way which made Daniel cringe and lurch farther away. "I just want my brain back."

Daniel decided not to stick around to try and understand what was happening but instead quickly reached for his pants with one hand while the other hand reached to unlock the bolt on the stall door. Randy swiftly took the opportunity to place his mighty hands on Daniel's head. He closed his eyes and, in deep concentration chanted, "Give me back my powers! Give me back my powers!"

"Get your hands off of me," Daniel shouted, opening the stall door but unable to fasten his pants at the same time. He struggled to get himself together so that he could escape.

"Just stay still and let me take back what is rightfully mine!" Randy shouted, as he climbed over the partition and into Daniel's stall, his hands still trying to grasp onto Daniel's uncooperative head. Daniel wriggled away.

"I don't have your *brain*! You are crazy!" said Daniel, finally able to hop from the stall, still wrestling with his pants which were coiled around his ankles.

"I'm not leaving without my brain," threatened Randy

who followed Daniel out of the stall. As soon as the self-help guru got close enough, he placed his giant hands on Daniel's head as Daniel continued to unsuccessfully attempt to unfurl his pants from his ankles. "I want my brain. I want my brain," Randy chanted, sounding deranged, his eyes closed tight as he struggled to concentrate and extract his mind.

In sheer desperation and barely able to avoid a full out panic, Daniel punched Randy's unprotected stomach for all that he was worth. With an, "Oof" and a deep groan, Randy let out a strangled shout and fell to his knees, winded.

Outside the restroom and down the corridor, Jack was helping himself to a bag of munchies from the vending machine when Daniel burst from the restroom, his pants still curled about his feet. Hopping a few steps, he fell to the carpeted floor.

"Hey, when I said hurry up, I didn't mean—" said Jack before he was interrupted.

"There's a crazy person after me... he's in the bathroom!" Daniel gasped out and pointed, now seated on the ground and finally able to pull up his breeches.

Jack produced what looked like a short billy club from seemingly nowhere and slowly pushed open the door to the men's room. "Was he armed?" he whispered softly and, it seemed to Daniel, quite happily. Daniel stumbled to his feet and followed close behind Jack.

"I don't know," whispered Daniel. "I don't think so."

When they entered the bathroom, there was no sign of Randy. "He said that I had his brain," explained Daniel, running what had just happened over and over again in his own mind, as well as giving more information to Jack. "He kept attacking my head with his huge, massive hands."

Seeing that the restroom was all clear, Jack looked out the other restroom entrance which led out onto a different corridor. The hallway was empty and Jack could see that it led directly to another street exit. "He's probably a few blocks away by now," Jack said as he returned to the bathroom. Not seeing Daniel, he turned around and searched the stalls and area by the sink. The bathroom was empty; Daniel, too, had vanished.

"Anybody got eyes on Spectrum?" Jack spoke into his walkie-talkie. Not receiving a response, he turned up the volume and spoke again. "Anybody there?" he asked. "All walkie-talkies should be turned on and operational until the director of security, that's me, tells you to turn them off. Over?" Again not receiving any kind of response, Jack pocketed the radio and exited the bathroom. "Amateurs," he exclaimed loudly as he kicked the trash can on his way out.

CONFESSIONS OF A FAILED NOVELIST

Daniel rushed out of the rear exit of the playhouse, and into the parking lot, where a car had to brake hard in order not to hit him.

"Are you okay?" asked Clare, rolling down her window. "I almost hit you!"

"Yeah, I'm fine," said Daniel, still clearly rattled. "My fault. I wasn't looking." Seeing Jack enter the parking lot from another exit, using Clare's car as a barrier, Daniel shielded himself from Jack's view.

"What's going on?" asked Clare, puzzled by his behavior.

"Trying to give my bodyguard the slip," he said, watching Jack with concern as he circled Daniel's parked car with interest.

"Are you not his employer?" asked Clare, questioning his logic. "Can I give you a ride some place?" she asked, realizing that Daniel seemed to have gotten himself into some kind of situation that he obviously wasn't sure how to resolve.

"That would be great," answered Daniel and sighed with relief. "Thank you," he said, sneaking into her car. "I seem to remember that I owe you dinner," he said, settling in.

Daniel and Clare sat across from each other in a cozy booth in a bar/restaurant, with a flat screen TV above the bar, not far from the playhouse. The more that Clare gushed effusively about Daniel's brain book, the more uncomfortable Daniel became. "I've been waiting all my life for someone to say the things that you say. It's like your book speaks directly to my soul, Charles."

Daniel fidgeted a long moment and looked around. "That's... terrific," said Daniel, motioning to the passing waiter. "Another double Scotch, please," he ordered and gestured for Clare to give her order, but she declined.

"Your book is a modern masterpiece. It's going to sit among the other major works of wisdom for centuries to come. You must feel so proud," Clare continued.

"Clare, the book isn't saying anything original. Trust me, it's a piece of crap," declared Daniel.

"How can you say that when the work has touched so many hearts and minds? That book has changed people's lives. It's a book for the ages."

"The book is a piece of junk. It's a satire. It was never intended to be taken seriously. People are idiots," said Daniel, clearly losing his patience. Puzzled and feeling a little insulted, Clare shifted as if to discern more fully his mood and method. Then she looked at him with renewed focus. He frowned with what appeared to be disgust.

"Are you toying with me?" she asked, tentatively. "Is this like a test, to throw my mind off balance, so that I can learn to see the real truth behind the artifice... or something?"

"Look, I'll be straight with you. Can I be straight with you?"

"Of course."

"I'm not who you think I am. For the past ten years I've written three wonderful books and I've struggled in anonymity; I might as well not have existed. To be totally honest with you, and I hate to say this or even admit it to myself, I'm... I'm what you would call...Despite the fact that two of them got published, I'm basically a failed novelist. There, I've said it." As Clare remained quiet and pensive,

Daniel did indeed feel better and his conscience was all the clearer for unabashedly and honestly declaring his hand.

"But your book is so... your talks are so... inspiring?" said Clare, totally confused and still expecting Daniel to say, 'gotcha' or deliver a punch line, and then perhaps tell her that he got her good.

"I'm doing all this for the money, actually. It's this or starve," confided Daniel, polishing off his drink and signaling to the waiter to order another.

"I don't know what to believe," Clare said, mentally defeated.

"Maybe I've been foolish and stupidly arrogant to think that I could follow in the footsteps of the great American writers but all I've ever wanted was to be taken seriously as a worthwhile novelist. The more I do this shit, the further away that dream becomes. Who's going to take me seriously now?"

"You are taken seriously," Clare argued, taking out her copy of the brain book. "This book has changed so many people's lives: the way they think, the way they relate to the world."

"I can't comment on other people's states of mind, that's for sure," Daniel said, accepting his new drink.

"Do good unto a good book and a good book will do good unto you," Clare quoted from the book with reverence.

"I would call that gibberish," Daniel smirked and slugged his latest drink.

"I took it to mean that if you really took in the words of an inspirational book... that true wisdom has a way of changing a person, from the inside. Haven't you ever felt changed just from reading a truly great book?"

"Of course," agreed Daniel. "But this isn't one of them, trust me," he said.

"People say that it's good to have an open mind but the best kind of mind to have is one that's totally vacant." As Clare quoted another passage, Daniel couldn't help himself and laughed out loud for a long moment.

"That's actually pretty funny," Daniel goofed, as if hearing it for the first time.

"But it's so Zen," Clare said earnestly. "The Zen masters would call a vacant mind, beginner's mind; which is looking at the world without judgment or preconceptions."

"I never read a book about Zen in my life," declared Daniel.

Again Clare flitted through the book and chose a quotation, "Before you say 'Yes' to life, make sure to see some identification."

And again, Daniel laughed. "You don't think that's funny?" he asked.

"Yes," agreed Clare with complete earnestness. "It's a very funny way of saying that you should approach life's major decisions, not always with a glib yes-to-life attitude as some would have you believe, but rather yes, with discernment."

"You have a knack for the elucidation of flippant jokes," suggested Daniel.

"Never open your heart before inquiring if there is an open heart surgeon in the house," Clare again quoted from the book.

"Yeah, see, that's just common sense," said Daniel, facetiously and chortled with glee.

"The open heart surgeon is God," Clare said with reverence and closed the book. Daniel abruptly stopped laughing and suddenly felt sober and chastened by her sincerity.

"Oh," he said.

"I find this all very confusing," admitted Clare.

"*You* find it confusing..." said Daniel, not finishing the thought.

"I don't know what to believe," she said, sadly.

"I'm sorry," said Daniel, feeling somewhat sad, himself. "This whole time has been... I don't know... surreal, to put it mildly. It's like I went to sleep one night and woke up the next morning in an alternate universe where everything was topsy-turvy; what I used to consider sane was now crazy and what was crazy was now... the height of wisdom or something. I'm sorry if I'm making you feel a bit foolish or humiliated, or both maybe, but if someone up there is playing a joke, then I'm not privy to it, either. I just went along with the madness, I guess."

"But what about your talks? I mean, they're wonderful. You don't seem to be making fun then... are you?"

Daniel thought deeply before answering. "I don't know but it's like the first time I stepped out on stage... in front of all those people, looking up at me with those hopeful, expectant eyes... like they're all hopelessly lost kids or something and for those few moments, I'm their one big hope... I guess, it's like I become someone else, maybe the way an actor feels going out on stage. I become who I think they want me to be; someone who they think has all the answers, someone who can give them guidance or direction, maybe. I've no idea what to say until I open my mouth to say something." Clare noticed that a tear glistened in Daniel's left eye. The teardrop hung there, perhaps awaiting permission to release, which he didn't grant.

"Call it acting, make-believe, or whatever you want," said Clare as she placed her hand upon his. "You have a gift, Charles. A beautiful, precious gift."

"I just feel so lost," Daniel said sadly, "so terribly, terribly lost and alone."

§

A very slick TV commercial played actual footage of Daniel, as Charles Spectrum, wearing his now familiar "power robes," talking to a packed auditorium.

"Charles Spectrum is a voice for the age," a deep, resonant male voice said. "Writer, teacher, mystic and prophet, his teachings have brought hope and joy to the thousands of people whose lives he has touched." The camera panned the attentive and adulatory audience as the narrator spoke.

"For those who feel lost... for those who feel helpless, in an ever-increasingly complex world, Charles Spectrum has a message." The scene shifts to outer space. The speaker's voice grew more resonant: "His words fill a space where before there was emptiness. His spiritual teachings reawaken dormant faith." An image, the brain book, appeared as a speck in outer space but then became magnified and filled the screen.

"His ideas shine a beacon of light into the bleak darkness of uncertainty." Another book appears before the first one, the title, *How to do Amazing Things Using Only Your Brain*.

"Now YOU can benefit from Charles Spectrum's amazing teachings. With clear and easy instructions on how YOU can find happiness; how YOU can achieve anything you set your mind to... *How to do Amazing Things Using Only Your Brain* and *You Have a Brain—Use it!* Available wherever books are sold."

Seated around a conference table, in Suzanne's agency, were about a dozen sharp-looking agent types. They applauded as Suzanne turned off the TV with a remote. Among the agents sat Clare and at the end of the table sat Daniel. In reaction to the proposed TV commercial, Daniel inwardly squirmed and outwardly found it hard to make eye contact with Clare. Based upon her facial expression, she also felt a sense of disgust. The agents turned and applauded Daniel, as if he'd had anything to do with it. He reacted with modesty.

On the rear of the meeting room's back wall was a large sign of a new corporate logo, a diagram of a brain and in block capitals, the name, BRAIN, INC.

"Great job, everybody. Love the music, Clare," said Suzanne, clearly relishing the entire project. "The commercial will be released to coincide with the launch of the new book," Suzanne announced proudly.

"Suzanne," interrupted Daniel, looking concerned. "I haven't even started on the new book and in truth, it may take me..."

"No problem," interjected Suzanne. "Take your time. We have a team of ghost writers working on books two and three as we speak. By the time you finish yours, it might become book five in the series," Suzanne joked, a few agents laughed politely. "You can relax," Suzanne addressed Daniel. "I know how much pressure we were putting you under."

"Oh. Okay," agreed Daniel.

"Frank," said Suzanne addressing one of the agents. "Why don't you tell us about the network?"

Frank rose from his seat and used a remote device to switch on a power point presentation. A large map of the USA was projected onto the screen. The detailed map was crisscrossed with color-coded cities and towns.

"We'll open offices and set up affiliates in all of the major cities. The staff will organize and book on-going seminars and regular classes in each of their territories. Plans are underway for similar operations in Europe and, eventually, most major countries of the world."

"The world?" Daniel blurted out. As the agents turned to him, expecting more, Daniel nervously smiled. "With all these seminars and classes going on... how can I be all over the world... at the same time?"

"We're recruiting other seminar hosts and training them... based upon your act, of course," answered Suzanne.

"Each of the seminars will be scripted," said Frank. "Every performer..."

"Every *teacher*," corrected Suzanne.

"Uh, yeah, every teacher will be saying exactly the same thing, the same kind of stuff that's written in the books," continued Frank.

Clare was the only one who appeared skeptical. She continually looked down the table to try and get a read on Daniel, attempting to discern from his reactions whether he was on board with the whole thing or not. Daniel, however, smiled nervously throughout and kept his eye line away from Clare, carefully avoiding any possible exchange of non-verbal communication via facial expressions.

"Tell them about advertizing, Matt," Suzanne addressed another agent, who stood up.

"Full media blitz to drum up advance bookings; book signings on both coasts, TV, talk shows..." Turning to Daniel, he smiled, "Again, don't worry about traveling."

"You'll book top acts," Daniel said and smiled, only Clare seeming to catch his intended sarcasm. "I'm confused, though," continued Daniel, "what *will* I be doing?"

"At this stage, the most valuable asset the company has right now is your name," answered Suzanne.

"Oh," said Daniel, not sure of the full implications of such a concept.

"Tell them about the merchandizing tie-ins, Sarah."

Sarah stood and held up some T-shirts. "We sell these at all the gigs," she began, and held an example up, and turned it, for all to see. On one side the T-shirt read: *I Was Lost But Now I'm Found* and on the back: *I Found Myself at a Spectrum Seminar*.

"We're placing the books across all media platforms: DVDs, CDs, MP3s and obviously all are available for instant download onto electronic devices. We're recording original music with Clare and performed by the Charles Spectrum orchestra, featuring the Spectrum Singers," continued Sarah, showing slides of the artwork to accompany the products.

"Then we have the "Reflections On Series, where Charles Spectrum will reflect on each of the star signs: Charles Spectrum on Sagittarius, Libra, Capricorn... all the signs of the zodiac. In another 'Reflections,' he will reflect upon crystals, aroma therapy and other healing methodologies..."

As Sarah continued at tremendous speed, Daniel, feeling greatly overwhelmed, found it hard to keep up.

"We'll have a nine-one-hundred number where people can call in for their Spectrum horoscope and a Spectrum Psychic hotline where people can seek advice... for an average call projected to bring in five dollars a minute when fully operational."

"Thank you, Sarah," said Suzanne. Then she lifted two large mail sacks onto the table.

"We're currently getting two sacks of fan mail per day," Suzanne declared. "That's a lot of names and addresses. Most of the reader's letters actually claim amazing results from using the techniques outlined in the book. We can use their valuable testimonials for advertizing in each of our territories." Suzanne looked at all the happy faces of the agents sitting around the table and smiled appreciatively. "Thank you all for your hard work," she said and noticed that Clare had her hand raised. "You have a question,

Clare?"

"Suppose these people are getting real results from the book? I mean, shouldn't we be researching that?" Clare asked, perhaps more for Daniel's benefit than expecting support or a positive reaction from Suzanne and the other agents.

"Good point," answered Suzanne. "However, as these claims are a bit on the outrageous side, psychic and paranormal phenomena are a little outside of our collective expertise. This team, and our emphasis right now is concerned with helping as many people as possible to benefit from Charles Spectrum's teachings. Thanks for asking, though."

"Sure thing," answered Clare as she looked directly at Daniel.

"Good meeting, everybody," announced Suzanne. "Bill, Matt, Sarah... my office."

Suzanne was the first to leave, followed by the enthusiastic agents. Daniel remained seated, looking a little shell-shocked. Clare stared at him. He was unable to look at her.

"Why are you letting this happen?" Clare asked softly.

Daniel didn't look like he had an answer and still avoided her gaze.

"You say that you've been ignored for years... that you were invisible, right?" continued Clare. "Now, when you've finally gotten people's attention... you sit back and let other people speak for you? I'm confused. What is it you really want?"

"All I've ever wanted was to stay home by myself, keep away from people and write books," Daniel said emphatically, finally making eye contact, perhaps wondering to himself how on earth he had ended up achieving the opposite of his inner desires.

"Then why do the seminars?" asked Clare, pointedly.

"If I can get enough money I'll buy a small publishing house and I can print and sell my books... any book I like. I'll be the boss and I won't have to deal with crass people, whose only concern is what percentage they can get for themselves and how they can use someone else to further their own careers," explained Daniel, vehemently, discovering, and surprising himself with the intensity of, his own inner resentment and anger.

"And what about all of the people that truly care and believe in Charles Spectrum?" Clare asked, looking at the sacks of fan mail sitting on the conference table.

"I don't know about those people," Daniel answered, not really wanting to know.

"What if you're not meant to be home alone? What if you're really supposed to be a teacher and you're just fighting it?"

"I really don't think..."

"Suppose there actually *is* something you don't know about... something unique inside of your book?" said Clare, persistent in her opinion. "Maybe people are tapping into some hidden power within themselves? What if your book was the most influential book ever written?" Clare asked pointedly and didn't seem too perturbed when Daniel audibly scoffed at the suggestion.

"Just think about this, for a second," Clare persisted. "If you wrote a book that you were proud about; some book that passed whatever yardstick you carry around in your head that said, yes, this is a brilliant book... and suppose that book generated just as much excitement as this book is generating... you'd be over the moon, right? You'd be savoring every positive review, reading every letter and email sent by appreciative readers... You'd probably be secretly believing that the book was indeed a masterpiece, just like everybody is telling you—"

"I'm not so— " interrupted Daniel, who in turn, was interrupted by Clare.

"You get bags of mail from devoted readers from all corners of the globe. Have you taken the time to even read any of them? Or are you too smug and superior to even consider it?"

"They're letters from..." started Daniel but deciding it best not to finish the thought.

"Letters from who? Crazy people?" asked Clare.

Daniel felt smaller and smaller in his seat. Clare slid a mail sack down the table in his direction. "Go ahead," she challenged, "read some."

Daniel looked at the mail sack before him and, reaching in, his facial expression suggested that he could just as easily be reaching into a bag filled with hissing vipers.

"You know what?" Clare suddenly declared, as if coming up with a different plan. "I have a better idea." Grabbing a mail sack with one hand and Daniel's hand with the other, she pulled him up out of his chair. "Come with me," she said.

GETTING TO KNOW THE CRAZY PEOPLE

Daniel drove as Clare sat in the passenger seat, sifting through the bags of mail.

"Too far… too far," she said, checking the return addresses of a handful of mail she had selected. "Here's one," she then said, recognizing the address as being local. She opened the envelope and took out the letter. "'Dear Charles'… that's you," she said to Daniel, smiling. "'This is going to sound really weird, or maybe not, but having read your book several times and done most of the exercises, I can now see spirits.'" When Clare stopped reading, Daniel gave her an "I told you so" look, which she didn't acknowledge.

"'I can now see spirits,'" she continued reading. "'In fact, my house has suddenly become haunted or perhaps it was haunted all along but only now do I notice it. What should I do to make them go away? Return the book, perhaps? Sincerely, Josh Madden' Gee," Clare finished.

Whereas Clare looked troubled, Daniel could barely contain his mirth. "This is your idea," he said, perhaps expecting her to call the whole thing off.

"Take the next right," she commanded. "Just because you don't believe in spirits doesn't mean that they don't exist," she said with seriousness.

As Daniel glided into the right lane, he didn't notice that the car behind, which also strayed into the right lane, was being driven by Jack. He had been following Daniel and Clare from the office parking lot. Nodding his head to the beat of his favorite rap music mix, Jack's eyes were so focused on following Daniel's car that he didn't notice that the car directly behind him was following him. It was being driven by a purpose-determined, Randy Guswhite. Driving the car with one-pointed concentration, Randy's large hands gripped the steering wheel so tightly that his knuckles were almost white in color.

"This is it," exclaimed Clare as she checked the address on the envelope with the street numbers of the affluent and historic homes in the quiet, Hancock Park neighborhood. Daniel pulled in and parked on the street. A few car lengths back, Jack pulled in behind some other parked cars. Unseen, Randy parked his car a few car lengths behind Jack.

In response to some tentative knocks on the front door by Daniel, a wizened old man peered from the slowly opening door, his eyes adjusting to the harsh, bright daylight.

"Mr. Madden?" Daniel asked.

"Yes?" answered the old man, cautiously.

"My name is Charles Spectrum. Sorry to show up unannounced on your doorstep like this... we happened to be in the neighborhood. Do you have a few minutes?"

"Charles who?" asked the old man, his rheumy eyes trying to focus on Daniel's face and, upon doing so, clearly not recognizing him.

"Charles Spectrum," answered Clare, sweetly. "The author. He wrote the brain book. You wrote him a letter," she said, holding it out for him to see.

"Oh, yes," replied Mr. Madden, it was all making sense to him now. "Please come in."

"You live on your own?" Daniel enquired as he took stock of the old world, cluttered and ramshackle interior which looked like it hadn't been cleaned in quite some time.

"I did until I bought your book, yes," replied Mr. Madden, somewhat cryptically.

"And now your house is haunted?" asked Clare.

"No!" Mr. Madden answered suddenly. "It's not haunted!"

"But, you did say in your letter..." Daniel cautiously stated and then exchanged a curious glance with Clare.

"I'm sorry I sent that letter," Mr. Madden said, emphatically. "It was a mistake. You should tear it up... forget I sent you the letter."

"There are no spirits, then?" Clare asked, hoping for some clarification.

"No. No spirits. You should leave now," he said, opening the front door.

In response to Clare's puzzled expression, which she directed to Daniel, Daniel shrugged his shoulders, as if to say that he was clueless.

"Promise me that you won't tell anyone about the letter?" Mr. Madden asked them as they stepped outside, back into the sun.

"We promise," agreed Clare.

"You' don't want people thinking that you're crazy right?" suggested Daniel.

"I don't want them to come take them away," replied Mr. Madden.

"Take who away?" asked Daniel nervously.

"The spirits?" asked Clare with more than a little certainty.

"Please!" Mr. Madden shushed them, closing the door behind him as he stepped out to join them. "They are very, very sensitive," he whispered.

"Oh," said Clare, now understanding entirely.

"Before they came, I was all alone," confided Mr. Madden. "Mrs. Madden has passed on this twenty years already."

"I'm sorry to hear that, Mr. Madden," Clare

commiserated.

"At first I was frightened... that's when I wrote that letter. But they are nice people; they are my friends now... no harm in them. I don't want them to leave, you understand?" Mr. Madden said, almost pleadingly.

"Sure, Mr. Madden," assured Daniel. "We understand. No one's going to come take them away."

"Wow," Daniel said as he and Clare returned to the privacy of the car. "What are you doing?" asked Daniel as he noticed Clare pick through the mail sack for other local addresses.

"I'm looking for another one," replied Clare.

"Another one?" asked Daniel. "Isn't one crazy person enough for one day?"

"Just because someone else's beliefs lie outside the limits of your beliefs and experiences, doesn't mean that they're crazy, Daniel" Clare said with sensitive seriousness. "To someone less mentally bright than you are, you could be considered a complete jackass."

"Note taken," replied Daniel, considering it a valid point.

"Let's go to West Hollywood," announced Clare, selecting another letter.

"West Hollywood, it is," agreed Daniel, starting up the engine and pulling out.

Behind Daniel and Clare, Jack pulled out and kept a modest distance. Behind Jack, Randy pulled out, also keeping a respectable distance.

Daniel and Clare were soon sitting across from Lisa and John Kukouski, a middle-aged, prosperous and equally overweight couple, in their tastefully furnished living room. The married couple was so very clearly in love and enthused about sharing their lives together that they were partial to finishing each other's sentences.

"Oh, sure, Lisa and I never did anything like this before, did we, honey?" John asked his wife as she came from the kitchen with a tray full of coffee and cookies for everybody.

"No, honey, never," Lisa concurred.

"A friend of hers read your book and..." started John.

"All of a sudden, she could see into the future, couldn't she, honey?" added Lisa.

"Just snatches here and there," agreed John.

"So I thought that that would be something I'd like to try and then John decides..."

"Well, seeing into the future isn't my thing but when I read that exercise on becoming one with nature..." John said.

"The one where you run around naked in the forest," clarified Lisa. "He used to have such a poor self image of himself. Not anymore..."

"Well, what do you know, but didn't we start seeing nature spirits..." said John.

"Elementals," corrected Lisa. "In the mountains up in the national park. Who'd have thought, right?"

"The secluded parts, you understand," added John.

"The pair of us, buck naked," Lisa laughed, then John joining in. "If my mother got her hands on this!" she said holding up a DVD.

"We made a video of one of our field trips," said John. "Would you like to watch it?"

"No, that's okay," answered Daniel, not even conferring with Clare. "We're good."

Despite Daniel's uncertainty and puzzlement regarding their meeting with the Kukouski's, as they walked back to the car, he felt more positive and upbeat, their ebullient energy and upbeat attitudes perhaps helping to raise his spirits.

"Okay," he admitted to Clare as they got back into the

car, "they may not be totally crazy, just a bit weird," he smiled.

"People seeing nature spirits, fairies and elementals has a substantial precedent and a long history among us human folk," Clare said with a smile. "Even some of the great poets and writers you admire wrote stories and poetry about them," she added, pointedly.

"Every north European poet from Chaucer to Yeats, it would seem," agreed Daniel.

"And let's not forget Shakespeare's *Midsummer Night's Dream*."

"Let's not," said Daniel, smiling. He looked like he was finally beginning to enjoy Clare's company. She smiled brightly into his eyes.

"One more?" Clare asked, reaching into mail sack.

"Sure," grinned Daniel. "Why not?"

An elegant lady in her sixties, of mixed ethnicities, Esther Woodbury lay wearing a swimsuit by the swimming pool at the back of her stately home. Her house was tucked privately away in the hills above Hollywood. Sitting as comfortably as they could, without lying down or falling off, Daniel and Clare shared a chaise lounge as Esther's personal maid served them each some chilled drinks in tall glasses.

"I read your book several times... thank you very much, by the way," Esther said, with gratitude. Daniel nodded his humble acknowledgement. "And now I can regress myself, unaided."

"Regress yourself?" asked Daniel.

"The past life exercise?" asked Esther, hoping to jog his memory. "Where you soak your head in ice water for four hours?"

"Oh. Yeah," said Daniel.

"I went back to first century Greece. I was quite the philosopher in that one," Esther smirked with the memory.

"I was a prostitute somewhere in Polynesia, 300 BCE, I'm guessing. Now that was an interesting one! I'm thinking of writing the biography on my life in that lifetime. That one will steam up the bookshelves, I'll tell you!" she laughed. "I'll use a pen name, of course. Couldn't use my real name or people will think I'm crazy, right?"

"Right," agreed Daniel.

"I'm sure you get that all the time?" she asked Daniel.

"All the time," answered Daniel.

When Daniel and Clare got back to the car, Clare looked at Daniel as if expecting a wise-ass comment. "Nice pool," Daniel exclaimed and smiled.

"Yes, it was," Clare smiled broadly. "Aren't you going to tell me how crazy she is?"

"Let's just say that for a crazy person, she seems pretty sane. And if she is crazy, it's working for her. She's doing all right for herself, wouldn't you say?"

"You think she's doing okay now, just wait till that book comes out," said Clare as she laughed, Daniel joining her.

"The weird thing is is that that stuff sells," said Daniel. "Erotica is right up there with the bible for number of units sold."

"No, it isn't," disagreed Clare.

"Pretty close," teased Daniel.

"One more?" suggested Clare, not wanting their time together to end.

"Seriously?" asked Daniel. When Clare looked at him with puppy dog eyes, he didn't argue one bit but turned the key in the ignition, instead. "One more. Then we're calling it a day," he agreed.

"Are you glad you're doing this?" she asked, another envelope at the ready.

"Yeah. I'm glad we're doing this," he smiled.

The last address they were going to visit was in a

neighborhood that neither of them were familiar with. The apartment building looked run down and, as they waited for the elevator, Daniel could distinctly smell something rotten. He kept his observations to himself. The door to apartment 206 opened to a crack when they knocked.

"Yeah?" a male voice asked.

"Hello, my name is Charles Spectrum and we're looking for Ray Buchwalder," said Daniel.

"That's me," the voice said as the door opened wider. "Come in."

Ray Buchwalder was a tall and mean looking character. He quickly looked up and down the outside corridor before closing the door behind them. As the door closed, Jack watched from the end of the corridor, his stocky frame obscured by some tall, leafy plants.

Noticing the filthy state of the apartment, Daniel and Clare exchanged glances which indicated their instantaneous shared speculation that maybe this visit wasn't such a good idea.

"You're the guy wrote the brain book, yeah?" asked Ray.

"Yes," answered Daniel. "We're doing a customer survey," he improvised. "On a scale of one to five, how happy would you say you have been with your purchase?"

"Fucking five, dude," Ray responded. "Are you shittin' me? That book blew my mind."

"A five, very good" Daniel said as he made a note on the back of an envelope. "Well, thank you for your time, Mr..."

"Call me Ray. The exercise where you jump up and down on the bed for six hours shouting, "I can fly, I can fly?"" Ray said. Daniel nodded and stood protectively closer to Clare.

"I did that for like three days straight and now my spirit

can leave my body and travel great distances, just like you said it would," Ray continued.

"That's great," answered Daniel, gesturing to Clare to move closer to the front door.

"Yeah, except now it's gotten me into a shit load of trouble."

"What kind of trouble, Mr... uh, Ray," asked Daniel, unobtrusively backing himself and Clare towards the door.

"Okay, so I'm in bed asleep at night. Then, my spirit body, you know, the astral double... it leaves my body and goes out somewhere, leaves the building, goes I don't know where."

"Yes," said Daniel, avoiding any questions or comments that would prolong their visit.

"So, next morning, I wake up and there's all these cops in here, guns drawn and everything. They arrest me, sons of bitches," exclaimed Ray, thumping the wall harshly.

"I'm sorry to hear that," said Daniel.

"They said I held up a liquor store. They said I shot someone! All the time I was sleeping!"

"I see," said Daniel.

"I told them that it wasn't me, that it was my astral double that done the stealing but they wouldn't believe me! I was in bed the whole time, I told them. We've got you on security camera they tell me. That's not me, that's my spirit body, looks just like me, a spittin' image, totally identical, right?"

"Right," agreed Daniel.

"They'll listen to you, guy. It was all your fault, after all."

"I don't think they'll listen to me. Cops think that I'm a real quack, you know? Zero credibility in the law and order department, I'm afraid to say," replied Daniel as he reached for the door knob, in preparation for making a quick getaway.

"Here, you can give it a try, anyway," Ray said, grabbing the phone from the wall-mounted cradle. "I got the cops on speed dial."

"We have to leave now," Daniel said as he took Clare by the hand and opened the front door.

"Not until you make the call," Ray said, shutting the door.

"I really don't want to get involved," Daniel insisted.

"Oh, you're involved alright, from the fucking get-go, you're involved, buddy," Ray said.

Without thinking, and truly desperate to leave, Daniel pushed Ray away from the door. He shoved him so hard, and so unexpectedly, that Ray lost his balance and tripped over a chair, and fell to the floor. "Hey, not cool, dude," Ray yelled.

Daniel quickly opened the door and pulled Clare out of the apartment with him. Once in the corridor, they ran like crazy, right past Jack who was still hiding. They galloped down the stairs to the safety of their car. Looking back at the apartment and seeing no sign of Ray, they exchanged nervous and excited looks with each other. Like two kids who had just outwitted and escaped from an angry adult, who was giving chase, they burst into laughter.

Getting to his feet, Ray did indeed give chase to the couple. Running out into the corridor, however, his path was blocked by Jack, who took the scruffy-looking angry dude in his stride. "Going somewhere, chief?" Jack casually asked, squaring up to Ray.

"It's a free country," said Ray. Ray took a step to his right, expecting to pass by Jack, but Jack moved, once again, to block his way. "Do I know you?" asked Ray, more annoyed.

"If you knew me, you'd remember me, trust me," said

Jack in his scariest, intimidating voice.

"Are you a cop?"

"Do I look like a cop?"

"Then get out of my way, douche."

"What did you call me?"

"You heard me."

As Jack and Ray traded barbs, and appeared to be about to break out into a scuffle, Daniel and Clare pulled out of their parking space. Behind them, keeping a discrete distance, was Randy. Driving past Jack's parked car, he decided that, like a fox, he had outwitted the guard dog and now had the run of the chicken coop. He smiled happily.

Daniel drove Clare to an address which she had indicated was her home. "You live here?" Daniel asked, pulling up in front of the small Spanish-style single story residence not too far from the Mid-Wilshire district.

"With my father," answered Clare. Something about the way that she said the word 'father' made it seem as if she were sad. Daniel picked up on it. "My father had an accident many years ago. It left him without the use of his legs."

"I'm sorry to hear that," Daniel commiserated.

"He has feeling in his legs but it's like he has this mental block," said Clare, who seemed to have some unresolved issues about the situation. "See, my mother was killed... he was driving. I think it's made him feel guilty."

"I'm sorry to hear about your mother," said Daniel, wondering if he should place a hand somewhere on her body as a sign of comfort and support.

"Is it like he's punishing himself by not walking?" asked Daniel.

"I want you to heal him," Clare said emphatically, looking him straight in the eyes.

"Come again?" asked Daniel.

"Look, I know that sounds crazy to you but hear me out," said Clare, close to tears but still displaying an inner strength. "I believe you have a gift. There's no question in my mind that there's something in that book. Sure, I know what your intentions were when writing it… but maybe you were in such a state at the time; not eating, not sleeping… You could have been in an altered state of consciousness, nearer to enlightenment, and not even have been aware—"

"I really don't…" interrupted Daniel, who was quickly interrupted by Clare.

"What if you tapped into a part of yourself, a much bigger part of yourself…"

"What is it exactly you want me to do?" asked Daniel, unsure about what they were even talking about.

"I want you to put your hands on my father and, with all the concentration you can muster, I want you to imagine that you can heal him."

"I'm not some kind of faith healer…"

"All I ask is that you *imagine* that you can heal him. There are no other expectations here. What's the worst that can happen? He's still in a wheelchair and you can go home and have a few beers and watch the game."

"Imagine that I'm healing him?" Daniel asked. The way that he said it made it sound like a concept which he was struggling to get his head around.

"Just pretend. Get out of your own way and just pretend that you have these miraculous powers. Not too different from a Charles Spectrum seminar, is it?" asked Clare, rather cheekily.

"Touché," replied Daniel, somewhat chastened.

"Thank you," said Clare, kissing him brightly on the cheek, which made Daniel smile and perk up. "I warn you, though," Clare said and stopped. "He's very cranky. Don't feel bad if he thinks you're a little kooky, okay?"

"I'm going to heal a crippled man with the touch of my hands and the power of my imagination. Why would he think that's kooky?" asked Daniel with a smile.

"You're a good sport," smiled Clare, getting out of the car.

As Clare led Daniel through the front door and into the house, Randy surreptitiously got out of his parked car and casually walked up the drive towards the rear of the house.

"Dad, this is Charles," Clare introduced her father, Tom. Daniel stood by the front door in the living room, shy and hesitant-looking. "Charles is going to make you walk again," she said boldly, not noticing the wince on Daniel's countenance as she spoke.

"Are you a doctor?" Tom asked Daniel.

"Uh, no," replied Daniel, wondering what he had gotten himself into.

"Charles is a faith healer, dad. He's going to heal you with his hands. Aren't you Charles?" Clare squeezed Daniel's arm as a show of support.

"I know exactly what he can do with hands," grumped Tom.

"Show some appreciation, father. Charles isn't getting paid for his time and purely wants to help you out of the goodness of his heart. Isn't that right, Charles?"

"That's correct," answered Daniel.

"So, go ahead and take charge, Charles. Tell my father what he needs to do for the healing to take place," Clare winked at Daniel. "He's all yours," she said.

"Very good," Daniel responded, looking around the small house, as if considering his options. "I need you be facing north, Tom," Daniel said, deciding that he had better display some take charge attitude and authority to prevent the cranky old man from walking all over him.

"Just let him try this for me, dad. Okay?" Clare said

sweetly, hoping to diffuse her father's stubbornness and lack of faith. "North is this way, Charles" she pointed. "Maybe we'd have more room in the kitchen?" she asked, noticing how the living room furniture was restricting her dad's movements.

Outside, at the rear of the house, Randy jumped a fence, his massive boots landing in a carefully manicured flower patch. Hoping not to be seen, his eyes fixed on the house, he trampled through the flower garden, devastating the delicate blossoms in his path.

With his back to the kitchen wall, at the rear of the house, Daniel stood behind Tom and placed his hands on Tom's head.

"She's had me stuck like a pin cushion and hypnotized and all kinds of... wacko psychics!" Tom blustered. "Herbal therapy, aroma therapy... and hot coffee up my ass! Damn quackery!" he exclaimed.

"Dad, it's really important that you relax or the energy transfer won't work. Isn't that right, Charles?"

"That's exactly right," agreed Daniel. "Tom, I need you to stay quiet for a minute, close your eyes and concentrate. I'm going to transfer the energy from my center to your head," Daniel calmly said, placing his hands back on Tom's head.

"I don't need it in my head," rebuffed Tom. "It's my legs that don't work!"

"Father!" chastised Clare. "How hard is it to close your eyes and be quiet for once?"

With their heads turned facing north, towards the front of the house, none of the three of them noticed Randy as he peered through a kitchen window. Randy, focused on how he could get his mighty hands onto Daniel's head for an energy transfer of his own and noticed a ventilation slit on the wall above Daniel. His scheming mind immediately concocted a plan.

Placing a wooden plank across two rain collection barrels, Randy carefully balanced himself on the plank. He then quietly removed the outside ventilation screen with his penknife and stood on tippy-toes to look through the small space. Seeing Daniel's head within arms' reach, he smiled broadly.

The front doorbell rang, causing Tom's eyes to open. "That's the UPS man," said Tom, seeing the outline of a brown uniform through the frosted glass panel of the front door.

"I'll get it," said Clare.

"Keep your eyes closed and concentrate on your legs," Daniel instructed Tom as he moved to the front of Tom's body and bent down to place his hands onto Tom's knees. "Are your eyes closed?" asked Daniel, his own eyes shut tight in concentration.

"Yes, my eyes are closed," answered Tom, "for all the good that's going to do me."

Choosing his moment and precariously balanced on the wooden plank, Randy stretched his arms out, into and through the ventilation space. Unable to see, coming out the other side, his hands flailed around, searching for Daniel's head.

"Do you feel anything?" Daniel asked.

"Of course not," Tom replied.

"You must concentrate. Place your hands on my head."

As Tom placed his hands on Daniel's head, Randy's hands found Tom's head and rested them there. Tom's eyes shot open, his body tensed.

"You feel something?" Daniel asked.

Outside, standing on the plank, his arms lost into the small space in the wall, Randy too had his eyes closed in tense concentration. "Return my powers, return my powers," he repeated over and over.

"Your hands are on my knees, right?" Tom asked
Daniel, trying desperately to keep his eyes closed, as
repeatedly instructed.

"That's where I'm sending the energy waves,"
answered Daniel, imagining in his head that powerful beams
of healing energy was shooting from his hands into Tom's
legs.

"It's like there's heat on my head," said Tom with a
look of utter amazement on his face. "It's like your hands
are on my head but I can feel them on my legs, as well.
You're good," Tom exclaimed, wondering perhaps if there is
something to this kind of healing, after all. "I can feel this
raging heat in my head *and* in my legs," he said excitedly.

"That's... it's working, then," said Daniel, masking his
own skepticism.

"The energy... the energy..." Tom proclaimed, as if
perhaps something miraculous was taking place. Unable to
stay seated any longer, Tom's eyes shot open and he
suddenly felt the urge to stand up. As he did so, Randy lost
his balance on the wooden plank and fell backwards into
the manicured flower bed. Neither Tom nor Daniel noticed.

"Sorry about that," Clare apologized upon her return to
the living room, "That parcel wasn't for us, after all. Dad,
what are you..?"

Staring straight ahead, like a man who just found
religion, Tom was almost standing erect. Daniel's eyes
widened in shock, his body frozen in amazement.

"Oh, my God!" exclaimed an astounded Clare. "He can
stand!"

Tom still had a tight hold on the arm rests of the
wheelchair but was almost fully erect, nonetheless.

"Holy shit!" Daniel blurted out.

His face a study in single-minded determination, Tom

let go of one of the arm rests and took a step forward. "He can walk! He can walk!" shouted Clare, beside herself with wondrous excitement.

"He can walk?!" Daniel asked and exclaimed at the same time.

Jumping up and down with complete amazement and joy, Clare grabbed Daniel in a joyous embrace, swinging him around. "You made him walk! You made him walk!" she repeated to a totally dumbfounded Daniel. Tom took a few more steps forward and then fell to the floor, the muscles in his legs too weak to hold him up. "Dad!" called Clare, going to his aid. As they both helped him back to the wheelchair, Tom displayed no signs of distress.

"I haven't been able to stand up in fifteen years!" he declared with undiminished wonderment.

Covered in dirt and assorted floral fragments, Randy wiped himself off and sneaked back over the wall and down the driveway to return to the cover and asylum of his black-tinted glass SUV. He watched as a befuddled Daniel left the house, accompanied to his car by an ebullient and supportive Clare.

"That was a wonderful thing you did with my father. I can't thank you enough," she said.

Seemingly speechless, Daniel repeatedly stared at his hands, turning them over and inspecting them, as if looking for clues which would shed light on what had just happened.

"Perhaps it's time to start finding out who you really are and where your power truly comes from, huh?" she said warmly.

"I guess," answered Daniel, his head a complete jumble.

"Drive safely, okay?" Clare said as she kissed him affectionately on the cheek.

WHERE THE POWER COMES FROM

Daniel was so wired, that he barely slept a wink all night. Thoughts swirled in his mind. Did he really heal a crippled man with the power of his own hands and mind? Scientifically, that would make no sense, whatsoever. Yet, his eyes didn't lie and unless Clare and her father, if that was her father, were playing some weird practical joke, what he had witnessed and was a party to could only fit into the fuzzy logic terrain of "faith healing." It was not an area which he had given much credence to in the past. What is *in* that book, he wondered. Were people really seeing nature spirits in the forest and remembering their past lives in ancient times and places? Were people becoming smarter?

More importantly, the fact that people were perceiving the exercises described in the book as being something which they should do to boost their brain power or whatever, was a disturbing notion. Whether or not they were getting results was not really the point: some of those exercises must be considered highly dangerous and potentially hazardous to people's health.

What is wrong with people, he thought. The "exercises" were obviously excessive and loony, who—in their right mind—would not find them hilarious in the extreme? Soak your head in ice water for four hours? Who on earth would read something like that and decide, yes, that's something I should try at the earliest opportunity? Jump up and down on a bed for days on end while constantly shouting, "I can fly, I can fly?" Was he the only one that saw the humor is such idiotic notions?

Aside from the fact that the person who actually

performed such a madcap adventure must have been psychotic to begin with, what of the people of sound mind who tried out these crazy exploits? Performing some of these brain-boosting exercises could definitely tilt the balance of someone who was already mentally on the edge of insanity and sink them right down into abject lunacy. If so, did he, as the author, carry any legal or perhaps moral responsibility? As is the case with the psychotic bed jumper, could other readers make a legitimate claim that the author is responsible for their mental states and their possible lapses into criminal activity, all the while using the excuse that "the brain book made me do it?"

What if people started jumping off buildings, thinking that they could fly? Or perhaps even walking backwards into the street and walking into the path of a speeding car or bus? Even if the book carried some caveat, or disclaimer, protecting the author, if such events begin to happen—and perhaps they already were happening—how could he assuage his own conscience and retire to his own soft bed at night and luxuriate in a peaceful sleep?

Even vitamins and food supplements that claimed to boost brain power were required to go through a lengthy experimental trial and seek governmental agency approval before they were allowed on the market. Shouldn't a similar type of procedure be considered for the brain book? Should the contents and the exercises, in particular, be exposed to rigorous testing before the book was deemed safe for human consumption?

The book needed to be recalled from shelves and download sites, he decided. All sales of the book must cease immediately pending an experimental trial period where tests were performed on the contents of the book to determine their suitability for an unwary public, particularly the mentally frail and unbalanced segments of society, of

DERMOT DAVIS

which there seems to be many. Daniel quickly left his bed, got dressed and left his apartment in a hurry.

Daniel decided to drive straight away to Suzanne's office. He was oblivious that he was being tailed by Freddie West, the *Inquiry* journalist. As he pulled his new Cadillac to the valet station in the underground parking garage and got out to be given his parking claim check, Carlos drove past him in another guest's car, then stopped, instantly recognizing him. "Hey! Pump the gas! Pump the gas!" he yelled at Daniel with a friendly smile and a wave. "Vroom, vroom," he mimicked a revving car engine. "Pump the gas, how are you?"

"I'm good, thank you," Daniel smiled back. "Got a new car," he gestured to his Cadillac.

"Nice wheels," Carlos said and whistled appreciatively.

"Have a good day," Daniel waved as Carlos drove away to park the guest's car. As Carlos found a parking spot and left the car, he was approached by Freddie, who detained him with the aid of a ten dollar bill. Freddie then took Carlos aside and asked him some pertinent questions regarding Daniel.

As soon as Daniel stepped off the elevator on Suzanne's floor, he noticed that the levels of activity had amped up greatly since his last visit. Interns and assistants ran hither and yon, frantically passing files, notes and information to each other and to the more senior agents. The phones rang non-stop.

Suzanne's office wasn't any different; Suzanne sat at her desk and took charge of the pandemonium like a commander of a war office. Assistants and staff came and went through the open office door, exchanging current updates and reports for new instructions from Suzanne. Undeterred, Daniel entered the maelstrom with unwavering conviction about his new purpose.

160

"Suzanne, do you have a minute?" Daniel stood at the door and asked.

"We've got a six minute segment on *News of the Weird,* Friday edition," a young intern reported to Suzanne.

"Good going," answered Suzanne. "Anything on ABC?"

"We can get on Josh DeLorian if we can find enough people who can do amazing things with their brains in like, the next three hours."

"Find them," instructed Suzanne. Matt left and Sarah entered.

"Another sold out seminar in New Hampshire," said Sarah. "We may need a larger venue."

"Draw up some options. Good work, Sarah," Suzanne made some notes. "Daniel," Suzanne finally acknowledged his presence. "Good to have you back. Where've you been?"

"I need to talk to you, Suzanne," said Daniel, fully entering with a greater sense of urgency.

"Shoot," said Suzanne as Sidney entered with a bunch of files.

"Hi, Charles," he greeted Daniel. Daniel waved back. "Suzanne, these letters need to be signed and sent out, like two days ago," Sidney said to Suzanne, opening up one of the files on her desk. "And *E! Entertainment* wants to know our current status on that reality TV pitch."

"I know about that," answered Suzanne while signing some letters. "I'm stalling to make them think we've got other suitors."

"Gotcha," said Sidney with a knowing wink. "And you know that they're waiting for you in the conference room, right?" added Sidney.

"Same principal, Sidney. Let them wait," Suzanne answered returning his wink. "You were saying, Daniel?"

"Two things," said Daniel.

"Walk with me," said Suzanne as she left her office in the direction of the conference room.

"Anything from Fox, yet?" she asked a passing Jamel.

"Not yet, Suzanne. I've got three calls in with them already."

"Call again," shot back Suzanne. "Keep calling till they either pass or say yes, okay?" Suzanne then turned quickly to Daniel. "What's on your mind, Daniel?"

"We need to recall the brain book and put all sales on hold, in fact, cancel the whole deal," answered Daniel, struggling to maintain his sense of certainty and urgency amidst the activity and craziness of the office.

"Frank, I need your decision on the NBC project. They're holding but they won't wait for long," Suzanne said to a passing agent.

"NBC is still my turf, Suzanne. We're doing it my way," answered Frank, tetchily and without breaking stride. Suzanne chuckled so softly that only Daniel could hear.

"You want to recall what, now?" Suzanne said to Daniel.

"The book," Daniel answered loudly. "We need to recall the book!"

"In here." Suzanne pulled Daniel into a side room which turned out to be a men's room.

"Suzanne, this is the men's room," Daniel pointed out the obvious. Looking around, he failed to notice a closed stall door underneath which a pair of feet was only obvious, if one was to look at the stall head on.

"It's empty. What's up?" Suzanne said.

"Suzanne, I want everything to stop, right now. The old book, the new book, the seminars... everything."

"Why is that?" she asked, biting her tongue and fighting hard to resist the urge to punch him hard in the face. She stared at his face.

"There may be something behind all of this, after all. I think I've tapped into something... something real. I think I may have made someone walk yesterday!"

"What on earth are you talking about?"

"Something's happened," he said, his voice full of emotion. He held up his hands with outstretched fingers. "I think I really do have amazing powers." His eyes were wide.

"Daniel, after the TV appearance, I want you to take a vacation, okay? I don't care where you go, I just don't want to see you hanging around, anymore."

"You think I'm nuts?" asked Daniel, outraged. "What do you mean, take a vacation? I'm Charles Spectrum. I'm the head of this entire enterprise. You work for me!" Daniel asserted himself. Misinterpreting her look of hatred and burgeoning anger as acquiescence, he puffed his chest out further. He stood taller and continued, thinking that it was high time that he put this woman in her place. "You're *my* agent and you do what *I* tell you to do. And I'm saying, time out, down tools... put a hold on everything until we assess exactly what it is that we're doing around here."

"Oh, shut up, you whiny little jerk!" Suzanne barked, her anger erupting. Getting up close to him, her finger pointed almost into his face, she backed Daniel all the way up to the rear wall as she spoke.

"Considering where you were, before you wrote this thing," she said, mimicking a suicidal noose tied around her neck, "you're doing damn fine. You didn't even know what you wrote until I turned it into something worth selling. Do you know how long I've waited for something like this? Something this big? You think I was happy being a failed novelist's agent, huh? Do you know how sick I am listening to you creative types whimpering and sniveling and moaning... Making excuses for your crappy work. 'Ooh, no one understands my staggering work of genius, I don't know why it isn't selling. Poor me. Ooh, I think I'm coming down with writer's block... Well, I'm sick of it," she exploded, completely backing him up to the wall.

"Whatever you have now right now is because of ME! It's a business, understand? And right now, you work for ME! Can I help it if you're too stupid to read a contract before you sign it? Huh?"

"What contract?" asked Daniel, weakly, pinned as he was, against the wall.

"The contract that said if you pull out, fail to meet the contractual obligations of Charles Spectrum, or do anything without express approval from the board, you forfeit all claims to any established or projected intellectual properties. In short, you will be penniless."

"What board?"

"Me!" Suzanne exclaimed.

"I signed that?" asked Daniel, vaguely remembering signing something when he received his first check for the brain book. Suzanne nodded. Daniel's face fell.

"Now," said Suzanne, backing off, her anger cooling. "It's very simple. Are you in? Or are you out?" She was sweating slightly, like a prizefighter closing in for the kill.

"I didn't know what I was signing," Daniel protested, feeling robbed and cheated. "You're my agent, for crying out loud. You're supposed to be the intermediary, looking out for me, looking after *my* best interest. Not yours!"

"Yeah, well... welcome to the real world, baby," Suzanne said, walking to the door. "I'll give you some money after the TV appearance. I suggest you go take a cruise or something."

As Suzanne left, Daniel kicked over a trash can in anger. He thought about what she had just said and, opening the door, he called after her, "What TV appearance?"

As he exited, the occupied stall door opened to reveal

a smiling Freddie, who appeared to have recorded the entire conversation on the cell phone that he was holding.

§

The slick TV daytime talk show host, Josh DeLorian addressed the camera, "People who can do amazing things with their brains and the man and the book that made it all possible... meet Charles Spectrum..." As the audience was cued to applaud, Josh turned to Daniel, who sat uncomfortably and uneasily in the guest chair.

Josh spoke directly into another camera, "A self-styled guru, who teaches that anything is possible if you put your mind to it, and three ordinary people who once lived ordinary lives... until they found Charles Spectrum's book." Two normal looking men and an average-looking woman sat in a row near Daniel.

"Meet Ricardo Morales," Josh said as he walked over to one of the men. "He was a successful but bored sanitary engineer."

"Janitor," corrected Ricardo. "It's okay to say janitor," he smiled. "I'm not ashamed."

"He was once a janitor," Josh continued, playing to the friendly audience, "but he has since quit his job and now plays the stock market." The audience applauded and, after waiting for the applause to subside, Josh continued, "He claims to be right *every* time, making money on *every* single trade... and he has the bank balance to prove it!"

The audience applauded; the applause grew louder when Ricardo unfurled a huge bank statement that looked like it's full of substantial deposits. Daniel hid his own surprise, not knowing the other three guests and, just like the audience, finding each guest's achievements a revelation.

"Meet Roger Jones," Josh announced, "an electrician who bought the book and soon thereafter, he threw away his toolbox. Oh, he still fixes electrical units but he doesn't have to open them up... he can fix them with his brain! Now his business is booked solid." The audience applauded wildly as Roger took a self-conscious bow.

"And finally," said Josh, moving towards the woman, "meet Sonya Carelli. Having read the Spectrum book, she has canceled her membership with four dating services because now she claims that she doesn't need them anymore... because she can now get any man she wants! Not only that but she claims to know every thought that her date is thinking, sometimes before he even thinks it himself!" The audience applauded as Josh straightened and addressed the camera face on. "People that can do amazing things with their brains... when we return."

As the set cameras switched off, the home TV audience was treated to a commercial break from the show's sponsors. Daniel squirmed more than ever when Josh casually introduced himself and told Daniel how excited he was to have an act like his on the show. "As a kid, I was a huge fan of Uri Geller," he confided to Daniel.

"That's... good to know," replied Daniel, not knowing the person that the TV host was referring to and not wanting to reveal his ignorance by asking who that was.

Watching the live show at home, Tom used the commercial break to go to the bathroom and Clare made some hot tea. As the kettle came to the boil, Clare heard a knock at the front door. When she went and opened it, Freddie stood before her, an innocent expression plastered across his face. "You don't know me but I'd like to talk to you about Charles... Charles Spectrum," Freddie said.

"Who are you?" asked Clare.

"Oh, I'm very sorry, I should have introduced myself

first," apologized Freddie. "I'm his father," he lied convincingly.

"Oh," extolled Clare, surprised but happy. "Come on in. We were just watching him on TV."

Back on the TV show, the electrician, Roger Jones stood before a table. Upon the table was a collection of electrical appliances: blenders, toasters, hair dryers, etc. Josh walked toward him as he addressed the camera. "Bear in mind that all of these appliances, although they are currently plugged in, our staff here have verified that none of them work." Turning to Roger, he extended his right arm in a sweeping gesture. "Roger, we challenge you!"

Roger placed both his hands upon a cake mixer, closed his eyes and appeared to concentrate very hard. To the audiences' amazement, the mixer roared noisily into life. The audience applause intensified, a few oohs and aahs were heard as Roger proceeded to go down the line and, by the same method, bring every single one of the broken appliances to life. Josh reacted with amazement, making a "Can you believe it?" facial expression for the benefit of the live audience and the audience watching at home. Daniel was equally amazed and wasn't quite sure how he was expected to react.

After another commercial break, Sonya amazed the audience and, it must be said, Daniel, with her mind reading techniques. Concentrating hard, she announced, "Payment." Josh opened a sealed envelope and surprised everybody by revealing that the word, Payment, was written upon it. "Amazing," Josh declared to a huge round of applause. "As well as attracting desirable people to you," Josh addressed Sonya, "you also say that you can get rid of people that you don't want around?"

"That's right," answered a cool and collected Sonya. "Whenever someone becomes too persistent, like a bad date or a bill collector," she asides to the audience, generating a laugh, "I just close my eyes, visualize the offending person and repeat the magic phrase." Raising her hands and holding them out, twirling her fingers like an amateur's magic act, she closed her eyes. "Trouble and strife, get out of my life. Trouble and strife, get out of my life," she repeated. "It's all there in the book," she confided.

The camera followed Josh as he turned to Daniel, hoping to catch his reaction, which was closeted befuddlement. "This stuff is amazing!" declared Josh. "We have thirty seconds. What does the author have to say?"

"Maybe I *was* in some altered state when I wrote it," exclaimed Daniel, more speaking aloud a thought than answering the question put to him in real time.

"Anyone can do this, regardless of age, sex, race, level of intelligence and so on?" asked Josh quickly.

"I guess so," answered Daniel, looking lost and at sea.

"Amazing!" declared Josh, once again.

"I guess so," added Daniel, completely lost for a meaningful response.

As Josh addressed the camera and said some closing words, thus ending the show, Daniel was ushered off the stage by a production assistant. "Josh would love to spend some time with you in the green room," she told him and quickly left in response to something she heard in her earpiece. Feeling inordinately hot, confused and secretly terrified, Daniel walked straight past the green room and off of the sound stage into the main building. Turning onto an office corridor, Daniel saw Suzanne, who was conferring with the three guests from the show. Breaking away from them momentarily, she greeted Daniel.

"Great job, Daniel," she said as she approached. "I think that went very well. Are you okay?"

"Who are those people?" Daniel asked, staring down

the corridor at the three performers that he just shared a show with.

"They read your book," she replied, matter-of-factly.

"Are they for real?"

"Here," said Suzanne, ignoring his question and reaching into her satchel, extracting an envelope. "There's twenty thousand in cash here. Seriously, take a vacation."

Without taking his eyes from the three guests, Daniel absentmindedly took the envelope from Suzanne. He noticed it in his hand only after she left him to return to the three waiting guests. Daniel watched them with interest, as Suzanne seemed to have given them each a similar-looking envelope. Suzanne promptly left. Daniel walked quickly to catch up with them before they reached the exit doors.

"Hey," Daniel shouted, as he approached. Only Roger turned to acknowledge Daniel, but the "electrician" didn't slow his gait, not wishing to engage. Daniel quickened his pace and, catching up with him, grabbed Roger by the arm. "All that stuff," said Daniel, trying hard to phrase an intelligent question, "all the electrical appliances and stuff... how did you do that?"

"Chapter six," replied Roger, breaking from Daniel's hold. "Become one with the machine. You know the exercise where you sleep with a toaster oven for six weeks?"

Judging from Daniel's expression, he had no idea.

"It's all there in the book, man," said Roger, pushing open the exit door.

"It works?" asked Daniel, looking forlorn as the exit doors closed in his face.

Suzanne met up with her brother, Jack, as he thumped a vending machine that presumably wasn't behaving as he expected. "Why aren't you baby-sitting Daniel?" Suzanne asked as she caught up with him.

"I don't want to do that shit, anymore," Jack replied, looking like he was having a very bad day.

"A minor altercation with a crazed fan and you quit?" teased Suzanne.

"I don't want to do this kind of work, anymore," Jack responded angrily. "You think I came all the way out here to spend my days and nights unwanted and disrespected as some two-bit bodyguard for an over-sized kid?"

"Jack, we had this—" Jack interrupted and Suzanne was not allowed to continue.

"I've been trying to tell you this since I got here but all the time you're too busy. When you said you'd give me a job, I thought, okay, I'll work in publishing or the movies or some shit, that'll be pretty cool. So, you make me wear a suit... but I'm still an ex-con doing a mug's job and still I'm doing the same kind of work I could have got for myself. It's bullshit."

"I had to consider your qualifi—"

"You're kingpin around here, right? Head of the outfit. You coulda given me any job you wanted." Jack stared meanly at his sister. She knew that he was right.

"Well, what job did you want?" Suzanne asked and sighed. She didn't need this right now.

"Okay, those guys are young and they got diplomas and shit. But they're not smart. They think that they're smart, but they're not smart... they don't know anything."

"You mean the junior agents? You want to be in on board decisions, is that it?"

"I don't want a muscle job I coulda got myself. For twice the money, by the way."

"Alright," acquiesced Suzanne. "Let me think about it, okay?"

"Get someone else to baby-sit the genius."

"Forget Daniel," said Suzanne, dismissively. "We don't

need him anymore, anyway."

"I thought he was the guru of the whole thing?"

"Let's just say that the organization has moved on and now he's just getting in the way. There's a saying in the publishing industry: "The only good author is a dead author." I had no idea what that meant up till now."

"You want me to help out with that?" asked Jack casually. It was a loaded question that Suzanne didn't fully recognize.

"I gave him some money to go take a cruise or something. I just want him out of the way, that's all," said Suzanne, taking her leave.

"Got ya," Jack said, a knowing look on his face and a sinister scheme forming in his head.

TROUBLE AND STRIFE

Freddie West sat across the desk from the editor of *The National Inquiry*, Carlton Weston. Looking distinctly depressed, and fairly overweight, Carlton was dressed in a cheap suit which was at least one size too small. Freddie sat uneasily and fidgeted obviously nervous and impatient, as Carlton finished reading his latest submission. "This is great writing, Freddie," Carlton said, finally. "Really exposes the guy as a fraud."

Freddie beamed a huge smile. After a lengthy bout with writer's block, he felt that this current exposé was the turning point in his stalled career that he so desperately needed. He knew that the work was good, that he was on to something, but hearing it from Carlton was huge satisfaction and a tremendous relief.

"It's too bad that we can't print it," declared Carlton, tossing the manuscript across the table towards an astounded Freddie.

"What?" asked Freddie, not quite sure that he had heard right.

"This is one of the best pieces you've ever written. It's well researched with cited sources; your interviews with all of the interested parties are informative and entertaining; it is overall, terrific journalism. We can't run it."

"I don't understand?" asked a befuddled Freddie, feeling shock, panic and anger, all at the same time.

"Who do you think reads the *Inquiry*?" asked Carlton, calmly. "The same people that read this book," he answered his own question.

"But, you just said—" blurted Freddie, lost for words.

"We'd be shooting ourselves in the foot printing that. Print tabloids are a dying breed, Freddie; no need to tell you that. Apart from losing the exceedingly valuable ad revenue that the Brain people spend with us on advertising, it would be like calling our own dwindling readership..." Carlton picked up the copy to find the exact quote, "complete imbeciles." Carlton looked at Freddie, who appeared as if his entire world had just caved in and he was about to start crying.

"Do you have anything else I could take a look at?" asked Carlton, hoping to bring the meeting to a close.

"I thought this was it," babbled Freddie, his voice quivering. "I mean, I spent so much time... I'm flat broke. Can't I even get something for my time?"

"I'm sorry, Freddie. You know how it is. We don't pay until we print."

"Things have been so bad for so long... I'm so behind on my mortgage that they want to take my house and I haven't paid alimony in so long, they're going to put me in jail... I really need this," said Freddie, his desperation making Carlton feel very uncomfortable. Carlton stood, signaling the end of the discussion.

"I'm sure something else will turn up, Freddie," Carlton said as he guided Freddie, who walked a funeral beat to the door. "Look on the bright side: you're writing great stuff again. I knew you didn't lose it."

"Yeah," replied Freddie, weakly.

Closing the door behind Freddie, Carlton suddenly looked troubled and weighed down by a dark and heavy depression which seemed to slowly engulf him. Quickly opening a filing cabinet, he extracted a bottle of whiskey and was about to pour himself a glass when an inner voice of reason stopped his impulse and had him intentionally reassess his actions.

Changing his mind, he returned the bottle of booze to its hiding place and, with a healthy resolve, he opened his desk drawer, where among a pile of Spectrum CDs and DVDs, he saw and picked up his well-worn copy of the Spectrum brain book. His hands shook. Among a plethora of color-coded page markers, he hurriedly flicked through several pages to select one in particular and like a junky about to get a fix, he opened the book to an oft-read page and began reading aloud.

"Just because I'm a good person that sometimes does bad things does not mean that I am a bad person," he repeated over and over. "My soul will not be burning in the fires of hell anytime soon, thank you very much!"

§

Tired, perplexed and ill at ease, Daniel drove towards his new condominium. Dreading the thought of walking into his empty and soulless, ultra-modern glossy high-tech home, he yearned for some warm, caring and understanding human contact. The only person that came to mind was Mavis.

Having not seen or contacted her in quite some time, he was excited at the prospect of seeing her again, yet he also felt guilty that he hadn't really thought about her much when he was busy and things were going in his favor. If anyone could provide an understanding ear and help him to better understand what was happening and, indeed, how to proceed further, Mavis was the top candidate. Remembering that this was one of the evenings that the library remained opened till late, Daniel made a course correction and headed for the local library.

Stopping at a familiar set of traffic lights, Daniel noticed his old car, the one that he had abandoned, on the side of the road. Covered in street dust and grime, it sported numerous police citations. As he made a turn towards the library, he passed the book store where he first met Randy Guswhite. The front window of the store was lined wall-to-wall with his brain book. A life-size cut-out of Daniel, as Charles Spectrum, greeted shoppers as they entered. Above the store was a large billboard that advertized the Spectrum seminar. *Feeling Confused and Lost?* it asked, then offered a solution: *Find Yourself at a Spectrum Seminar.*

Once inside the library, which was about to close for the evening, Daniel approached the reference desk. He was disappointed not to see Mavis' smiling face as he had been mentally visioning her welcoming countenance and her customarily warm greeting.

"Hi. I'm looking for Mavis," Daniel addressed an unfamiliar face. There was a female librarian, whom he didn't know, seated behind the desk. "Is she working tonight?"

The librarian stopped what she was doing and gave Daniel her full attention. The serious way with which she looked at Daniel caused him some premonitory anxiety. "Mavis is..." started the librarian and then decided to change tack. "Did you know her personally?" asked the librarian.

"Yes," replied a now concerned Daniel. "We were the best of friends, as a matter of fact. Is everything okay?"

"You haven't heard, then?" asked the librarian, now feeling very uncomfortable.

"Haven't heard what? Has something happened?"

"I'm afraid that Mavis passed on several weeks ago," answered the librarian, becoming aware that this was likely very bad news for Daniel to hear and that he might not take it well. "I didn't know her personally, but I believe the cancer that she had been battling with for so long finally overtook her," she said. "I'm terribly sorry."

"She had cancer?" asked Daniel, shocked, upset and confused.

"That's what I heard," replied the librarian, wondering to herself just how well this young man had known the deceased, after all.

"I didn't know that she had cancer," Daniel said, more as a thought meant only for himself than as a comment to be shared. "She never once mentioned it."

"She had it for quite some time, I believe," the librarian added, just as the lights began to be turned off and a voice announced that the library was now closed and that all patrons must leave.

"Thank you," said Daniel dizzily, not fully cognizant of the huge shock that he was actually experiencing. "Thank you very much."

Daniel drove back to his home in a mental daze, his mind replaying all kinds of random memories of Mavis, none of which he seemed to have any control over, just as he seemed to have no control or knowledge of the tears streaming down his face. What bothered him the most was that he was one hundred percent sure that she had never mentioned that she was battling with cancer, or indeed acknowledged any kind of suffering or ailment, in all of their shared time together.

Did I ever ask, he wondered to himself. Had he ever even inquired about her health or her welfare or indeed anything in her life with which she may have been struggling? Had all their talks and their coffee meetings been all about him and his travails; him coming to her with problems in his life to be solved and she acting merely as his confessor, guidance counselor and confidante? It was horrible to conclude this yet, as per the random recall of his memory, it seemed to be true.

The realization and admittance of his abject selfishness

and downright lack of care and compassion filled him with self-loathing and made him sick to his stomach. What kind of a caring, loving human being do I take myself to be, he asked himself. What a true failure of a human being I have become, he deduced; a shockingly sad, hopelessly lost, miserable excuse of a man and downright waste of a heavenly apportioned, compassionate soul, I am. I absolutely hate and detest myself, he decided. Feeling utter despair, he drove back to his condo.

Just as Daniel entered his still unfurnished residence, his cell phone rang.

"Hello?" he answered.

"You don't know me," Freddie said, disguising his voice and calling from a pay phone outside his regular dive tavern in Hollywood. "My name is Bo Cartwright. I'm a private detective."

"Yeah?" said Daniel, his own problems to solve depleting his reserve of social tolerance and godly patience.

"I'll get straight to the point," said Freddie, sensing his mood. "I've got information about you that could put you in jail."

"What are you talking about?" asked Daniel, very close to hanging up.

"Impersonation with intent to fraud is a federal offense."

"I don't know what you're talking about," answered Daniel, his harsh resolve beginning to weaken.

"I think you do, Mr. Waterstone," said Freddie, pointedly. "As well as looking at two to five in the penitentiary, I print what I've got on you and no publisher would want to know you, ever... period. In short, you'll never get published again!"

"Wait a minute," said Daniel, his thoughts still coming to terms with what might be transpiring.

"Call me at 555-3249 at midnight and I'll tell you how much and when," Freddie said and quickly hung up.

Daniel just had time to write down the number and, putting the phone to his ear, didn't hear anything at the other end. His phone rang again. "Hello?" he answered.

"It's Clare," a soft voice said.

"Boy, it's good to hear your voice," Daniel said, his body temporarily relaxing.

"Are you okay?" asked Clare, hearing the angst in his voice.

"No," answered Daniel, quickly. "I just found out that my best friend... my only friend died weeks ago and I was too selfish to even..." Daniel choked up and couldn't finish the thought.

"I'm so sorry to hear that, Charles. It sounds like it was—"

"I think I'm losing my mind," Daniel continued, as if he didn't even hear Clare speak. "I may have these amazing powers; I have no idea what's in, never mind, who wrote my book; I'm stuck in a contract I signed that gave away all my power and now I'm being blackmailed. I may be going crazy."

"Blackmailed?" asked Clare, with concern.

"Which could seriously jeopardize my writing career. Oh, Clare, you know so little about me. My real name is Daniel," he said, feeling instantly cleansed at the revelation. "Daniel Waterstone. I used to—"

"You used to write darn good novels!" Clare said, looking at his two published novels which lay on her lap. "*Heartache* is such a beautiful, wonderful, amazing book," she beamed, using every glowing adjective that she could think of.

"You found out? Who told you?" asked Daniel.

"Your father," answered Clare, stroking both his novels

with a sense of awe and reverence.

"My fa-father?" asked Daniel with complete bafflement.

"He came to see me."

"My father's been dead ten years," exclaimed Daniel. "Wait a minute," he then said, his head now so confused, he was liable to consider any notion, fact or fancy. "My father came to you?"

"He told me all about you," Clare spoke gently, "what you were like as a child... He said that you hadn't spoken to each other in a long time but he was still keeping an eye on you. He seemed very concerned about you. Asked me lots of questions."

"My father *appeared* to you?" Daniel said, more a puzzled statement than a question. As if unable to mentally process anything further, Daniel absentmindedly hung up and placed the phone on his only chair. He stared into the mid-distance, as if incapable of sorting out his thoughts and unable to reclaim his sense of self. Only when the phone rang again, did he realize that he had just hung up on Clare, mid-conversation.

"I'm so sorry, I didn't mean to hang up on you like that," he quickly spoke into the phone.

"That's okay, Mr. Spectrum," a gruff, male voice responded. "How would you like to make front page news on every newsstand from here to—"

Not letting whoever it was calling to finish, Daniel hung up and put his phone on silent. As if losing the power to stand on his own two feet anymore, his body fell into his armchair. It was the only item of furniture which he had brought with him from his smaller apartment. Staring out of the window, looking at the shadows made from the adjoining tree branches in the declining light, his mental gearbox down-shifted into neutral, where no thoughts were noticed, either coming or going. It was in this frame of mind that he drifted into a deep, dark sleep.

§

Jack consulted his open laptop for instructions while constructing a home-made bomb at Suzanne's kitchen table. Having spent some years in the army and many more years being affiliated with an underground paramilitary militia group (which concerned themselves with the resistance of what they perceived as the increasing corroding of individual freedoms by the federal government, in general and in particular, its unremitting assault on the second amendment right of each citizen to bear arms), he was well versed in urban guerrilla warfare tactics.

He made his bomb with great love and an elegance of movement that was almost beautiful in its precision. Placing the compact explosion device into the innards of a nondescript, generic clock radio, he smiled with pride.

§

With admirable concern, Clare repeatedly dialed Daniel's phone only to go have it go straight to his voice mail, each time. Trying for the last time, and, once again, not being able to reach him, she placed the phone into her lap and considered her next move. With increasing concern for Daniel's welfare, she decided that a personal visit to his new apartment might be the best course of action.

He had sounded confused and stressed out of his mind. Even if he wasn't considering doing something that involved a noose, or taking an inordinate number of sleeping pills, surely a visit from a caring human being would provide a calming effect. At the very least, it would give Daniel some amiable company, a real human interaction from someone who cared enough to listen to him as he talked out his thoughts and troubles. Then and there, Clare decided to call Suzanne's personal cell phone number and ask for Daniel's home address.

Still slouched in his beloved armchair, Daniel abruptly awoke from a disturbed sleep. He had been in some hellish netherworld which he hoped he would not have to revisit any time soon. Disoriented, he looked around at the bare walls and room, relieved to be there yet still feeling, at heart, painfully bereft. Switching on a light, he checked the time: 11:15 PM. Remembering that he had a phone call to make at midnight, despite feeling stressed, he thought things through. He first made a mental metaphorical road map in his head of what he was facing, with the blackmail, and what he should expect to encounter.

The blackmailer, a certain Bo Cartwright (likely not his actual name, Daniel decided), would invariably give him a time and place to drop off some money. Most likely, it would be a demand for cash, which, luckily, thanks to Suzanne, he was in possession of. However, as with most, if not all cases of blackmail which he had read about in books or seen portrayed on TV and in film, the blackmailer, despite promises to the contrary, would most probably return again and again looking for more and more money.

How to avoid that situation and have it be a single pay-off scenario now preoccupied Daniel's thoughts. If he could discover the true identity of the blackmailer, then he could find some leverage to bargain with, such as going to the police and revealing to them the whole sordid plot, identity of the criminal, included.

Daniel quickly searched for the phone number he had been given, on an internet search engine, to see what would come up. It turned out that the results were nothing useful. It's probably a pay-as-you-go phone that criminals use for a job and discard soon after in order not to be traced, he figured.

Although it wasn't the appointed time, Daniel decided that he would call the number. Perhaps he would get lucky. Maybe the call would go to the person's voice mail where he might reveal his real name, if he wasn't a very bright criminal, that is. In truth, the guy had sounded exactly that: a not-too-bright criminal. Daniel dialed and, listening to the repeated ringing, waited for a response.

Unbeknownst to Daniel, he was calling the street payphone outside a dingy bar on a side street in Hollywood. A passerby in his forties, who either had a call to make or was just passing by, got curious and picked up the ringing telephone. He listened.

After what seemed like an age, Daniel heard the phone get picked up. He waited and listened for a greeting of some kind. When he realized that the person on the other end of the line, if there was one, might be doing the exact same thing, Daniel broke the silence. "Hello?" he asked tentatively.

"Hello," replied the passerby, with similar circumspection.

"Look, I know that it's not yet midnight but maybe we can work—"

"Hello?" interrupted the man.

"Mr. Cartwright?" asked Daniel.

"Who?" responded the man.

"Bo Cartwright?"

"You have a wrong number, pal," said the man, relaxing into the situation. "This is a pay phone."

"Wait a minute; don't hang up," implored Daniel. "What's the location?"

"Corner of Hollywood and Mayfield," said the man, quickly and just as quickly, hung up.

Not trusting his current state of mind or his short term memory, Daniel wrote down the street intersection. Checking the exact current time and mentally computing how long it would take him to get to the address in question, Daniel considered that if he rushed, he may just make it in time to get there before midnight and maybe approach the blackmailer in question.

Or, then again, maybe not, he determined; what if the criminal was armed and became abusive and threatening at having his identity discovered? Perhaps Daniel should watch him from a distance and then determine a plan of action but then again maybe he should decide on a plan of action, right away. There were many permutations and each of them overwhelmed him.

The whole, troublesome conundrum stressed Daniel to his mental limit. A myriad of thoughts, worrisome, and detailed horrible scenarios flooded and crisscrossed his already over-loaded brain. Amidst all the mind-melting cacophony, one thought exploded into his mind and in an instant cleared out every other thought that was bouncing around within its confines: what if he really did have amazing powers and he could deal with the blackmailer just like Sonya Carelli dealt with unwanted suitors and bill collectors, as she had so clearly demonstrated on national TV?

Grabbing his eReader, plus the envelope of cash which Suzanne had given to him, Daniel placed the cash into a sports bag and hurried out the door. His haste, and his unfamiliarity with the complicated high-tech locking system of the front door to his new pad, ensured that he failed to lock it securely.

From his stake-out car, positioned outside Daniel's

apartment, Jack quickly put aside his soda and fast food and picking up his potentially explosive clock radio, pressed the timer button, which started a 30 minute countdown. He then scurried out of his car. As he rushed towards the author, Daniel quickened his step to reach his parked car.

"Hey, Daniel. Wait up!" called Jack.

"Look, I don't want a bodyguard tonight. Take the night off," said Daniel.

"Relax," replied Jack, catching his breath. "I just came round to say goodbye."

"Oh?" said Daniel, pleasantly surprised.

"Suzanne tells me that you're going on a long cruise or out of the country on a vacation or something," Jack said, fishing.

"No," replied Daniel, somewhat puzzled. "I'm not going anywhere and as a matter of fact I'm in a rush, so if you wouldn't—"

"Isn't that your car being towed?" Jack asked quickly, looking past Daniel, as if seeing something of importance. As Daniel turned to see where Jack was indicating, Jack quickly slipped the clock radio into Daniel's sports bag. When Daniel failed to see that any car was being towed, he turned his gaze to check on his own car and make sure that that was indeed his own car that he was walking toward.

"Pretty sure this is my car here," Daniel answered and indicated the vehicle with a wave of his arm.

"Well, take care of yourself," said Jack, retreating. "You won't be seeing me again."

"Are you quitting?" Daniel asked, surprise in his voice.

"Done with the whole body-guarding shit. Take it easy," concluded Jack, now rushing back to his car.

"You too," said Daniel, not quick enough to say it within Jack's earshot.

As Jack and Daniel pulled out in their respective cars,

each going in opposite directions, Clare arrived and parked in front of Daniel's building. Quickly entering the newly-built condominiums, rather than wait for the elevator, she trotted up the stairs. When knocking on his apartment door and then calling his name produced no reply, Clare became increasingly anxious.

When she turned the knob and the door freely opened, her initial surprise and relief was quickly replaced with concern about what state she might find him in, upon entering. Unconsciously holding her breath, Clare looked into each of the empty and unfurnished rooms of the apartment. When she failed to find him, her contracted lungs sent a message to her brain. With immeasurable relief, she deeply inhaled a much welcome breath of fresh air.

However, Daniel's absence remained a puzzle, which she hoped to quickly resolve. Looking around the apartment for clues, she spied a piece of paper on the floor. It had the words "Phone booth, Hollywood and Mayfield" written on it. Not knowing what else to do or where else to look, she decided the clue provided was the next lead to follow. To that end, she hurriedly left the building.

Freddie West entered the phone booth at Hollywood and Mayfield and nervously checked his watch. As soon as he did so, the telephone rang and his body jumped from the unexpected fright. Taking a good hard deep breath, he picked up the phone. "Yeah?" he answered with the toughest, most disguised voice he could muster.

"Bo Cartwright?" asked Daniel who sat watching him from his parked car and was calling on his cell phone. Squinting his eyes hard, in the lamplight-lit semi-darkness, he attempted to mentally catalog every identifiable feature of the blackmailer's body and visage. Unfortunately, all Daniel could see was his back.

"Okay, here's my terms," began Freddie. "Fifty thousand bucks and I go away, for good."

"Look down at the floor and you'll see a travel bag," Daniel instructed. Freddie now noticed the bag which was tucked into a dark corner of the booth.

"Yeah?" asked Freddie, not knowing what to make of this new development.

"There's twenty thousand dollars in there," Daniel said, quite calmly. "That's all the cash I have. Take it and promise me that you'll leave me alone."

Rummaging through the bag, Freddie was pleased with the bundles of cash yet obviously displeased with the amount. Puzzlement, over seeing a clock radio among the cash caused little response beyond an imperceptible shrug of his shoulders. "This isn't enough," Freddie barked but really didn't know how to proceed.

"It's all I've got. I'm not with Brain Incorporated anymore and I'm not entitled to any more funds. Take it or leave it."

As if now realizing, for the very first time since he hatched and executed his illegal scheme, that what he was doing was wrong, Freddie's conscience woke up. He had a sharp realization that he was basically a good person doing something bad. Confused for a moment, he wasn't quite sure how he ended standing in a phone booth outside of his regular watering hole extorting a bag of cash from an author of literary fiction and a runaway best-selling, self-help manual.

"Look," Freddie said with a measure of desperation, not realizing that he was forgetting to continue to disguise his voice, "I want you to know that I don't normally do this. In fact, this is my first time. It's nothing personal... just been down on my luck lately, well, for quite some time, actually—"

"Forget it," Daniel interrupted, uncertain if this sudden mood of contrition was part of the unknown blackmailer's act or if he should give him the benefit of the doubt and assume that the guy was now being genuine. "I know how desperate people can get when things don't work out. If things don't go our way consistently, over a prolonged period of time, I have no doubt that we are capable of doing practically anything and whether such acts born of extreme desperation are legal or illegal sometimes bears no self-recognition or concern. In such a state, I firmly believe that any man is capable of doing almost anything."

Daniel's words struck such a vein of recognition within Freddie that, unbeknownst to his conscious awareness, tears formed in his eyes.

"You're such a nice guy, I hate myself for doing this," Freddie announced with painful remorse. "If I didn't need this money so bad... This is the last you'll hear from me, I promise," he said and quickly hung up.

Daniel put his cell phone away and switched on his eReader. Selecting the brain book, he left his car and followed Freddie at a discreet distance. Quickly searching for a specific chapter in the book, he found the passage that Sonya had shared, which apparently had been extremely successful for her purposes.

"Trouble and strife, get out of my life. Trouble and strife, get out of my life," he repeated, putting the book away and twirling his fingers in Freddie's direction like a cliched villainous magician from an old Looney Tunes cartoon.

Daniel didn't pause in his chanting as Freddie entered a bungalow-style house in the quiet, predominantly working-class, ethnically diverse neighborhood.

"Bad vibes, bad vibes, bad vibes," he continued as some passersby gave him wide berth. When a loud explosion ripped through Freddie's bungalow, shattering windows and setting off car alarms in the otherwise quiet neighborhood, Daniel's body froze, his jaw dropping to its limit, his eyes staring and opened wide. "Oh, my god!" he said out loud. "Oh, no! Oh, please, no!" he stuttered, terrified and panicked at the sudden drastic and frightening turn of events.

As people appeared from all directions and clustered among themselves, asking each other unanswerable questions, Daniel once again, raised his arms and twirled his fingers in the direction of the destroyed and burning house. "I didn't mean it! I take it back! Zap! Everything's fine! Zap! Everything's fine!" he repeated.

Having lost her way several times, Clare finally arrived at the intersection and immediately noticed the emergency vehicles and flashing lights a few blocks away.

As emergency personnel wheeled Freddie's body out on a gurney, Daniel walked alongside, his magic fingers extended towards his blackmailer's still breathing body. "You feel great! You feel great!" Daniel repeated.

"Sir, please stand back," a police officer blocked his path.

"You never felt better! You never felt better!" Daniel shouted at Freddie as he was being taken into an ambulance.

"Behind the tape, sir, please," insisted the officer.

"I need to be with him. I can make him better!" implored Daniel.

"Are you a doctor?" asked the skeptical officer.

"No. But I do have amazing powers," answered Daniel in abject seriousness.

"Behind the tape, please," the officer responded.

Seeing Clare arrive, Daniel's eyes and body lit up. "Clare!" he called with mounting joy. "How did you... Look, I blew up a building!" he pointed both horrified and impressed.

"Come with me," Clare linked his arm, pulling him away.

"I caused a huge explosion!" Daniel protested like an overly tired small child.

"There's nothing more you can do here," she said calmly. "Come with me. Everything's going to be okay." Taking him to her car, putting him inside and carefully buckling him in, she swiftly drove from the scene.

THE HUMAN ACHE

The more that Clare took charge, the more that Daniel began to relax. She drove them off of the city streets and onto the freeway. "You sounded so terrible on the phone," Clare said, not taking her eyes from the road ahead. "And when we got disconnected... well, I didn't know what to think," she explained. Noticing the lack of response and sensing that Daniel was simply staring at her, caused Clare to feel uncomfortable. "What?" she asked, and quickly glanced at him.

"Nobody's ever believed in me the way that you seem to believe in me," he said, his facial expression one of child-like vulnerability. His voice was husky with emotion.

"I do believe in you, Daniel," Clare confirmed as she placed her hand on his and squeezed softly. As they drove in silence, Clare soon realized that Daniel had fallen asleep. When she reached their destination, she parked slowly and evenly so as not to waken him. Looking at his sleeping face, his head tilted against the headrest, she felt very caring and protective towards him; almost a maternal feeling, she thought to herself. She gently woke him by placing her hand to his soft cheek. He opened his eyes and looked around.

"Where are we?" he asked, unfamiliar with his surroundings.

"We're parked outside my studio," she answered quietly. "No one will find us here."

They left the vehicle, Clare leading and Daniel following, and entered her place. Daniel marveled at the amount and diversity of musical instruments which were housed within Clare's surprisingly large studio. "Do you play all of these?" he asked.

"Only in so far as I can measure their authentic sounds against the instruments that I use when I compose music," Clare answered. Seeing the perplexed expression on Daniel's face told her that she didn't answer his question to satisfaction. "I compose on this," she explained, switching on an electronic keyboard which was connected to a computer, an amplifier and a host of large speakers. "Meet my orchestra," she said, sitting down at the keyboard and playing a beautiful chord that sounded just like a piano would sound.

"Music soothes my human ache," she confessed.

"Your human ache?" asked Daniel, not sure if he heard her right.

"The feeling you get when you come back to an empty apartment after a disappointing day and there's not a soul to greet you?" Clare asked, hoping for some recognition and acknowledgment from Daniel. "The ache you feel in your heart when you spend Christmas alone?" she tried again.

"The anti-climax I feel when after many years I finally finish writing my book and I've no one to celebrate with or no real friends to replace the characters in my book who have, for that short time that I was writing, become my friends," Daniel concurred. Clare smiled happily. Each of them understood the other perfectly.

"Want to hear how I compose my music?" Clare asked.
"Sure."

"Just like us, all that musical notes really want to do is find their way home," Clare began.

"Okay," encouraged Daniel, not really understanding what she way saying.

"Home is harmony," continued Clare, "where they start out from. The chord C, for instance." Clare played the C chord. "Peaceful. Cohesive," she smiled. "But then the time comes that, for whatever reason, we have to leave that home and all that we know." Clare played a beautiful melody. "At first, it's a lot of fun... getting drunk, partying, enjoying all kinds of sexual escapades..." Simulating a symphony orchestra, sounding just like an over-the-top orchestral soundtrack, she played a happy, somewhat choppy, melody to accompany her commentary.

"You have all kinds of interesting and madcap adventures... highs and lows; sorrows and joys... until you begin to realize that it is all spiritually empty and ultimately, dissatisfying. All the party people that you thought were your friends, you soon discover, care little to nothing about you. You've spent all your money on good times that, in retrospect, were not good times at all and now you have nothing to show for your time spent in hedonistic pursuits..." As she spoke, she played beautiful music... wild, delicate, jarring, evocative music.

Daniel watched Clare navigate the keyboard like the sublime master that she was; the music affected his emotions, each note related to her discourse. He had never been so spellbound by a woman before, or indeed by anyone, quite like this.

"And then you begin to feel lonely," Clare continued, the music becoming solemn and suggesting introspection. "Outside, you notice that it is appearing to get dark and you are now aware that you are cold and hungry... Home is looking far more appealing to you now, but you're far, far away from home." The music grows more urgent, as does Clare's commmentary.

"All you can see is darkness; everywhere is dark and scary... and you're all alone. The wind blows harder. Strange, threatening-looking forms appear all around you. You don't know what they are but you know that they are malicious and mean you harm... so you run. You run hard and you run scared. You run this way and that way..."

It sounded as if there were a real-life orchestra in the room. Daniel was totally caught up in the music and the story, as if a movie were playing in his head. If he closed his eyes, he could imagine himself sitting in a darkened movie theater where he was so familiar with the story and the characters that he knew every frame.

"Running blind," Clare's voice conveyed a sense of urgency and fear, "you don't know where you are or where home is or even if you're running in the right direction. Can't anyone help direct you towards home? Can't anyone show you the way? Can't anyone come to your aid and save you?"

Just then, as if having reached a crescendo, the music shifted to one of sadness and melancholia. "You stop running. You stop because you are tired and worn out. You haven't got anything left. You are so beat that you fall down. You are weak. You are exhausted. It is only then, that you listen. Within the chaos of the discordant din, you sit quietly and it is only now that you begin to hear, to truly hear that one sound which you never listened to before, though it was always present."

As if from the orchestral gloom, a sole instrument, perhaps a viola, sounded a solo tune. Weak at first, it strengthened in tone and volume and as it increased in strength, it suggested happiness and lightness above the murky gloom of the other heavy and depressing-sounding instruments.

"As you listen to that one sound, you begin to block all other sounds out, until that one, happy sound, is all that you hear. It speaks to you in a language which you don't know but that mysteriously, you can now understand. As you listen to its whisperings, the way home is revealed. It doesn't tell you or even show you a map. It is in the listening, that you discover which way it is you must go. You now know which is the way home."

Clare ended the entire piece with a melody that smoothly transitioned into the key of C and she finished - just as she began - by playing the chord of C itself, the final chord of her arrangement. For Daniel, the resulting quiet was highly charged. He felt like he had just been on an emotional roller-coaster, taking the exact same trip which Clare had related, without leaving her studio.

"Wow," was all that he could manage to say.

"That's the power of music," Clare said, smiling inwardly with pride. "What you're feeling now is exactly why they pay big money to have large orchestras accompany the movie story as a film soundtrack. Good composers know how to influence the emotions with music. By choosing which instrument to play which melody and in what correct tempo and even at which volume to play it, they can evoke sorrow, excitement or happiness in an audience."

Clare smiled and shifted her position in her seat, as if having a realization. "I'm sorry," she said, "I can get so caught up in music and composing sometimes. It's probably only very interesting to me..."

"Are you kidding? That was amazing," replied Daniel, still captivated. "Did you just make that up?"

"You want a copy?" Clare asked, reaching across him to press a button. Daniel watched enthralled as a hard copy of the musical arrangement came gliding out of the laserjet printer. "I'll leave the title up to you," she said, and handed him the printout.

"Clare's theme," Daniel decided instantly. "Symphony of the heart."

"You want to hear the real symphony of my heart?" asked Clare, playfully. She didn't know what overcame her.

Something about the moment, sharing her art with him, elicited a joy and playfulness that she hadn't experienced around Daniel before. Without waiting for a verbal response, Clare took Daniel's head and gently pulled him towards her so that his left ear was now pressed to her heart. "Do you hear it?" she asked.

"Yeah," replied Daniel, playfully. "Ta-rump, ta-rump, ta-rump." Daniel lifted his head, his cheek just grazing the bare skin - skin not covered by her clothing - of Clare's chest and shoulder. "It's beautiful," he said, looking intently and amorously into her eyes. As their eyes shared an everlasting moment of fused intimacy and longing, their bodies slowly leaned towards each other until their lips merged in a passionate and mutually besotted, romantic embrace.

§

Daniel and Clare woke up the next morning, their arms and legs entangled as they lay in a makeshift bed in a corner of Clare's music studio. "Good morning," whispered Clare, with a broad smile of absolute contentment.

"Good morning," whispered Daniel, returning her smile. As if then thinking that there was something vitally important that he needed to find out, he asked, "Are you still levitating?"

Clare made a little noise and smiled, just quietly and broadly enough not to classify as a laugh. She ran her fingers through his tussled hair. "It stopped the day I met you," she replied.

"Were you really... levitating?" he asked, like this was very important for him to know.

"I think it was just a recurring dream," Clare said, still trying not to break into a laugh.

"Why are you on the verge of laughing?" Daniel asked,

not wanting to treat the serious subject with undue levity.

"I had to make up something as an excuse to invite you to lunch, didn't I?" responded Clare, playing with his ear lobe.

"Are you kidding? I would have gone to Paris with you that day, had you simply asked. You made the whole thing up?"

"Like I say. It was probably just a recurring dream I was having."

"Oh," responded Daniel, his mind reconfiguring multiple layers of interconnected thoughts based on this new information. Daniel sensed that there was more to the story than simply a ruse to invite him to dinner. He also felt that in some way she was perhaps protecting him and not sharing fully for fear of over-loading his already panic-stricken mind with further complications.

"Does that change your whole opinion of me now?" prompted Clare, sensing his thought process. "You assumed all along that I was a crazy person?"

"Just a little," responded Daniel, his mood lightening.

"You're a wonderful writer, Daniel Waterstone. Do you know that?"

"Too bad nobody buys my books."

"They just need to be promoted."

"Tell me about it," responded Daniel, his own thoughts, exactly. As if a magic spell had been broken, and the harsh reality of his situation came flooding into his brain, Daniel's whole demeanor changed from happy and relaxed to panicked and anxiety-ridden.

"What are you going to do?" asked Clare, staying horizontal as Daniel got up and searched for his clothes.

"If that blackmailer is dead, then I'm a murder suspect."

"Call the hospital and find out his status. He's probably

just fine."

"They won't give that information over the phone," Daniel thought out loud. "I'll need to go visit."

"Do you have time for breakfast?" asked Clare, now rising from the makeshift bed.

"Probably not. I need to do something about Suzanne and Brain, Inc." pondered Daniel, his mind running through a 'to do' list for the day. "They need to be stopped; that whole brain book put on hold," he reasoned.

"Stop them, how?"

"I need to go public as Charles Spectrum and declare the book and the whole outfit as a fraud. If the guru exposes it all as totally bogus, then it's game over for that book and for Suzanne."

"And for the person formally known as Charles Spectrum," added Clare.

"Yep," said Daniel, smiling. "Him too."

AMAZING REVELATIONS

Suzanne slammed down her coffee in anger, some of it spilling on the morning edition of the newspaper on her desk. The newspaper headline read: *Mystery Explosion in Hollywood, Police Puzzled*. Jack was summoned before her, his attitude akin to a naughty pupil being called into the principal's office.

"You stupid idiot!" yelled Suzanne, her face red with rage. "Don't you realize that you've jeopardized the entire organization? Huh? You think I've built up this company so you can... so I can join you in jail?"

"How did you know it was me?" asked Jack in almost a little boy's voice.

"Because when I opened my laptop this morning it opened up on some weird how-to-make-a-homemade-bomb page!"

"You said you wanted him out of the way," responded Jack, weakly.

"Out of the way in... Hawaii or a cruise in the Bahamas or someplace, you idiot!"

"If you're firing me, you have to pay severance," Jack casually decided.

Suzanne looked at him with a mix of incredulity, contempt and absolute disgust. "Get out!" she yelled. "I still haven't decided yet if I should turn you in to the authorities solely on the grounds that you are a menace to society."

Suzanne's phone buzzed. "Charles Spectrum on line two," announced Darlene. "Are you in, Suzanne?"

"Yeah, I'll take it. Put him through," Suzanne answered on speakerphone, while shooing Jack away with her hands.

With a serious pout, Jack turned and left. "Daniel," Suzanne said brightly, "Where are you? Are you alright?"

"We need to talk," Daniel said curtly.

"I would love to," responded Suzanne sweetly. "You can swing by, anytime."

"The Sunset Room at noon," Daniel said and quickly hung up. With a perplexed look on her face, Suzanne extended her arm and displaying a sudden burst of anger, swept the entire contents of her desktop flying across the room. "I *hate* authors," she bellowed.

§

Daniel entered the hospital where Freddie West was being treated. He approached a stern-looking woman in her forties who sat behind the reception desk. A man, who sat holding up a newspaper in front of his half-concealed face, watched Daniel with significant interest.

"Hi," Daniel greeted the frowning receptionist, who didn't return his smile. "I wonder if you can tell me how a patient is doing... Frederick West." The receptionist looked up at Daniel but her silence, demeanor, and lack of otherwise meaningful response, caused him to be even more nervous than he already was. "I'd just like to know how he's doing... his current status," Daniel continued, "Freddie West."

"Are you a relative?" she asked.

"I'm his son," Daniel lied, expecting the question.

Typing the name into a search field on her computer, the receptionist waited for the results. "They transferred him out of intensive care," she then reported. "He's in Ward C on the third floor."

"He's okay, then," Daniel commented. "If they transferred him out of intensive care, it must mean that he's out of danger, right?"

The receptionist looked at Daniel with greater interest, a suspicious look breaking out on her face. "He's now in Ward C on the third floor," she said sharply. "You can ask about his condition when you get there."

"I'm not here to visit," explained Daniel. "I just needed to know how he is doing. How pop is doing."

Her eyes narrowing, the receptionist adopted a highly suspicious-looking demeanor. "Why don't you want to go up and ask him yourself?" she asked.

"I don't have time to visit," responded Daniel, trying to sound casual. "Will he be okay?"

"You don't have time?" the receptionist asked with puzzled alarm. "Your father just managed to survive with his life and you can't give him five minutes of your precious time?"

Increasingly uncomfortable, as the receptionist seemingly took a personal interest in his affairs, Daniel wondered if he should leave. Noticing that the man with the newspaper appeared to be taking an interest in him, further triggered his emerging paranoia. "I have to be somewhere," Daniel explained. "I have a meeting."

"You don't care, do you?" asked the receptionist, her voice laced with derision.

"Excuse me?"

"How many times did you visit him when he was healthy?" asked the increasingly agitated woman. "When you had the time? What? Maybe once a year, if he was lucky?"

"Well, no, as a matter of fact..." Daniel stuttered, completely thrown by her questioning and at the level at which she seems to be taking his business personally.

"Your type makes me sick," the woman exclaimed, not even trying to mask her personal hurt. "He gave you the

200

best years of his life; probably holding down two jobs, working his fingers to the bone, sending you to the best schools and the best colleges... and for what?"

"Thanks very much for your help," Daniel interjected, backing away and hoping that his retreat would cue her to stop talking. "Take care," he waved.

"He gave you the best education that money could buy just so you could get some yuppie, high-paying job and did you ever thank him? Huh? You never even once thanked him, did you? Your type makes me sick." Daniel didn't turn back around to acknowledge or respond in any way to the receptionist's tirade. He quickened his step as he got to the exit doors. The man with the newspaper casually got up from his seat and surreptitiously followed him.

§

The interior of the Sunset Room was dark and filled with red vinyl booths. The décor made it seem like an ideal kind of place to conduct an extra-marital affair. Suzanne sat waiting in a booth near the rear. She waved when she spied Daniel enter and look furtively around.

"Okay, I'm not getting into a big discussion about this," Daniel spoke quickly, eschewing any kind of greeting and hoping that if he stuck to a prepared speech, he wouldn't give Suzanne room to try and persuade him otherwise, which she would invariably try to do.

"Daniel, I'm so terribly sorry!" Suzanne shot up from her seat. "I want to apologize for my brother's behavior. I knew absolutely nothing about it. I swear to God, I had nothing to do with it."

The sudden and unexpected confession from Suzanne threw Daniel for a loop. He looked annoyed that he had to stop and think about what she had just said. "You knew nothing about what?" he asked.

"About the bomb. He acted on his own initiative, the idiot."

"Who did?"

"My brother. Jack," responded Suzanne, now realizing that Daniel had no idea.

"Your brother planted the bomb? Why? Was he trying to take out the blackmailer?"

"What blackmailer?"

"The guy in the hospital," answered Daniel, becoming more frazzled.

"The bomb victim was blackmailing you?" Suzanne asked.

"Why did your brother plant a bomb?" asked Daniel, his head now swirling with new information to process.

"Never mind about all that," said Suzanne with a swift wave of her hand. "I know that you're going to go on television and expose us all as frauds."

"How did you—" Daniel began, his whole rehearsed speech now gone out the window.

"The TV people called us to confirm your appearance."

"Oh," said Daniel, mentally kicking himself for not thinking of that possibility.

"You don't have to do this, Daniel. There is another way."

"I'm listening," responded Daniel, lost for any other kind of response.

"Two million dollars," said Suzanne with an ease and coolness that helped make the offer seem very appealing.

"Two million dollars," responded Daniel.

"Two million dollars," repeated Suzanne, really milking the sexy allure of it all.

§

"Two million dollars," Daniel later repeated to Clare at his apartment, although he couldn't quite replicate the teasingly tempting tone with which Suzanne had proffered the offer at his earlier meeting. "Two million dollars and they'll leave us alone, for good. No strings attached."

"So, instead of exposing them..." Clare said, beginning to understand but not appearing to like what she was hearing.

"We just walk. Two million will buy that publishing house I've always wanted."

Clare remained silent but it was clear that she was very dissatisfied with the fact that Daniel was even considering the offer.

"Clare, I know what it's like to be without money," Daniel said, in his own defense."To walk away from all of this... and to have the funds to allow me..." Daniel stopped when he saw that tears were welling up in Clare's eyes. Judging by her demeanor, she was not open to shifting.

"Taking this money is just another lie. Haven't you lied enough already?"

"Clare, it's easy for you to take the high road. You don't know what it's been like."

"The person that wrote that book said that what matters most in life is, "Truth, integrity and hope." I believed what you wrote in that book, Daniel, even if you, the author, doesn't. Maybe that qualifies me as just another looney." Clare opened the door to leave. "Say what you like on TV today but I'll never stop believing."

As Daniel watched Clare leave, he wanted to call her back and tell her that the money didn't matter and making her happy was worth more than any number of millions that he was tempted with... but for whatever reason, or sets of reasons that he was unable to identify, he couldn't. Two million dollars was, after all, a heck of a lot of money.

§

Randy Guswhite sat on a bar stool in his local dive bar and nodded to the bartender for yet another beer. The TV got his attention. More specifically, it was Daniel's photograph with a voice-over announcement about an upcoming broadcast of the Josh DeLorian show which caused him to stand on his feet with a mix of curiosity and anger. "Turn up the TV," he yelled.

"Today on *Josh at Three*," a male announcer excitedly shared, "Amazing revelations from Charles Spectrum, the author and self-styled guru. We are rescheduling our planned show to bring you the Spectrum interview live..." When the bartender returned with Randy's drink, he was surprised to discover him missing.

§

Freddie West lay in a hospital bed, watching the exact same TV commercial. Barely recognizable, his body was so comprehensively covered by a full body cast, surgical tape and bandages, that he resembled an embalmed Egyptian mummy.

"That murdering son of a bitch!" he managed to say, even though it hurt like crazy. Mustering all his strength, and propelled by anger, he tilted and swiveled his restrained body off of the bed, hoping that contact with the floor would aid in propping him erect enough that so that he could finish standing upright. Against all the laws of gravity, he managed to get to his feet.

Reminiscent of a B movie monster, he took one comical staggering goose step after another and left the hospital room and ward.

§

Daniel sat uneasily on the studio set as the production personnel rushed around and busily prepared for air time, which a count-down timer indicated was two minutes away. Standing off to the side, Suzanne stood watching. Close to her, Jack and two tough-looking buddies of his kept an eye on the goings on, surreptitiously watching for any signs of trouble or possible disturbance.

Historically for Suzanne, even though she sometimes wished that her brother was not in her life, she would invariably invite him in when she required tasks that only someone of his ilk could provide. Apart from serving her own needs, she considered that, as they were family, she could at least throw him a bone every now and then. It was almost her only way of expressing sisterly love toward her wayward brother.

Suzanne smiled at a nervous Daniel and, with the hand that didn't have their fingers crossed, she signaled him an A-Okay gesture. Josh DeLorian appeared and stood ready to address the camera just as the on-air light came on.

"On our show today, startling revelations from Charles Spectrum and his brain movement!" Turning to Daniel, he made sure a camera got a clear shot of his guest. "Charles Spectrum, you called our office saying that you had some very surprising things to tell us about your best-selling book and your organization?"

"That's right, Josh," Daniel answered.

"Join us, when we return," Josh announced into the camera and instantly relaxed when the show went to a commercial break.

While eating their lunch, Clare and her father watched

the show with interest.

While the cameras were down on the set, a make-up person fussed with Daniel's hair. The man who was pretending to read the newspaper at the hospital previously, entered the studio with two other cop-looking types. When challenged by a production assistant, they each flashed their badges and were speedily allowed entry.

Randy Guswhite arrived at the studio entrance but held back when he saw that it was guarded by beefy studio security personnel. Watching the crew guys enter without being challenged, he got an idea. He walked back down the street to an under construction building. He ambled along the chain-link fence on the edge of the site, out of view of the crew, then covertly picked up a roll of heavy-duty cable that was lying around. Carrying the roll of cable on his shoulder, he casually strolled past the studio guards, who wrongly assumed that he must be a member of the crew.

The on-air light turned to red and Josh addressed a camera. "Welcome back. In the studio we have Charles Spectrum." He then turned quickly to address Daniel. "Getting right to it. Mr. Spectrum, you have some startling revelations to tell us?"

The camera moved so that Daniel's face filled the entire frame. His internal dilemma showing on his face, he seemed unable to form any words. Josh waited. Suzanne and Jack exchanged a worried glance. The three cops split up, each taking an area of the stage to establish their presence.

Watching Daniel's frozen face on their large flat screen TV, Clare could barely watch, let alone eat. "He'll do the right thing," Tom said, patting Clare's hand as a show of support. "He has an honest face."

"Mr. Spectrum?" Josh finally cued Daniel.

"Yes?" answered Daniel, as if interrupted from a deep

trance.

"This is live TV, Mr. Spectrum. Startling revelations?"

It was as if Daniel could feel everyone holding their breaths as he took a deep one. "Brain, Incorporated..." he began and stopped. "...is a greedy, unethical company that's bilking innocent people out of their hard-earned cash."

Unlike Jack, who looked so angry that he could smash Daniel's face in, there and then, Suzanne looked disappointed but not too terribly surprised.

Clare heaved a huge sigh of relief and allowed a huge smile to break across her face.

"The organization is actually run by opportunists and ex-cons. It's a huge hoax," spoke Daniel as a healthy color of pink returned to his cheeks and his body relaxed from the stranglehold of truth withheld.

"Low-life, double-crosser..." Jack said as his zero-tolerance for snitches and dirty, yellow-bellied rats instinctively prompted him to pummel Daniel into a bloody mess. Heading for the stage, he was stopped by two production personnel. Sensing his mood and seeing that Jack's two cronies were stepping their way with purpose, as well, they radioed in for serious security backup. Anticipating the trouble that was to ensue, Suzanne quietly slipped away.

"Why declare this now, when you have so much to lose?" Josh asked Daniel.

"I used to think that there were basically two types of people in this world: normal people and crazy people. I now realize that there is just one group of people. Everybody is crazy; we're all just crazy in different ways. We each have a different kind of crazy," explained Daniel.

Unbeknownst to Daniel and Josh, a scuffle had broken out between Jack and his two cronies and a recently arrived security guard. The senior cop signaled to the other two cops not to interfere, just yet. Randy Guswhite stood in a darkened area and, biding his time, watched everything with interest.

Sitting before a panel of TVs in the TV control room, the small staff of producers wondered to themselves what the backstage disturbance might be. "What the heck is going on out there?" said an executive producer into his headset.

"The management from Brain Incorporated want to beat up Spectrum on the air!" a voice answered. Thinking quickly that, on the one hand, the unexpected development could be tragic, the producer also realized that the developing situation could also be great TV.

"If they interfere with the cameras, we'll cut to a commercial. Otherwise, keep the cameras rolling," he instructed.

A taxi pulled up to the TV studio and, with great effort and in almost unbearable pain, Freddie West was helped out of the cab. Looking like he had just walked off a movie set, which the appropriate title might be, *The Mummy Returns,* Freddie ignored the flashing On-Air red light and entered the studio, without incident.

"So, what I hear you saying is that the whole world is crazy and there's no such thing as sane?" asked Josh.

"Perhaps there are varying degrees of crazy, I don't know. All I'm saying is that I'm not in any position to judge. All my life I thought that I saw the world correctly and everyone that didn't see the world in the same way that I saw it, was... to all intents and purposes, insane. To many other so-called sane people out there, I'm sure they would consider me somewhat crazy."

"I can attest to that; I've read some of your book's reviews. What about your book? By your own admission, you considered yourself to be among the sane. Why did a sane person write a crazy book?"

"Perhaps because of the fact that I was in denial of any madness within me," Daniel said contemplatively, "...and maybe what I did was put all my repressed madness into that book. I don't truly know what was going on in me at the unconscious level."

"What do you have to say to all those people who bought your book and, as a result, believe that they can now perform miracles?"

"Can people talk to spirits and fairies and, as you say, perform miracles? Sure, why not? I'm in no position to judge."

"What, would you say, contributed to your change of heart?"

Looking directly into the camera, Daniel addressed Clare directly and spoke from the heart. "I need to thank the woman in my life for showing me how to accept and indeed, how to love and embrace my own madness."

Clare watched Daniel on TV with absolute delight, tears streaming freely down her face.

The fracas between Jack's men and the studio security personnel escalated. Punches were thrown and bodies were being bounced against cameras and sets as things got out of hand.

Freddie staggered in. With one arm outstretched, he purposely goose-stepped towards Daniel. "I'll kill him. I'll kill him," he murmured to himself.

Inside the control room, the producers were panicked, every one of them arguing among themselves and shouting into their headsets trying to get some reliable feedback from the set. No one answered as every able-bodied assistant was in some way involved in the skirmish, attempting to restore order. All the television screens before them displayed just one image: that of Daniel's face, as if only one camera was still working. "We keep rolling," the executive producer instructed.

Oblivious to the madness around him, Daniel continued talking directly to the TV camera. He didn't even notice when one of the cops handcuffed him to the chair which he sat in. Making his move, Randy calmly strode onto the set right behind Daniel and placed his massive hands on Daniel's head. Closing his eyes in concentration, Randy chanted out loud in an attempt to regain what was stolen from him. "Return my powers. Return my powers," he repeated over and over.

"There's lots of madness out there," Daniel continued, still undeterred, "and maybe we should stop looking at our supposed differences and instead realize that perhaps the one thing that we truly have in common *is* our madness. Maybe it's our craziness that is the one thing that makes us human, after all."

Clare watched Daniel with pride and increasing love and respect. From the corner of the screen, Freddie appeared, his arms outstretched, walking towards Daniel like a demented mummy robot. "Oh, my God," declared Clare, squinting her eyes to get a closer look at Freddie's half-covered face. "I'd swear that that's Daniel's father!"

"He looks like one of those mummies you see in the museum," commented her father.

"You're right, he so does. He's been dead ten years," announced Clare, oblivious to the perplexed, double-take expression which her father gave her in response.

Clare's eyes were fixed on the screen. She reacted with shock when Freddie tripped on some cable and fell, seeming to have disappeared as quickly and in as ghost-like a way as he had initially appeared. "He's disappeared again," exclaimed Clare. "That is *so* weird." Tom kept an eye on his daughter, wondering if perhaps she was finally, really and truly, losing it.

When the TV show returned from a commercial break, what was displayed on screen was a standard running of the end credits sequence with a voice-over announcer explaining how potential audience members could get tickets for an upcoming taping of the show.

§

When the backup request was finally answered, by the local police station, all of the outside visitors to the TV set were rounded up and taken to a large holding cell where they were left to wonder about their arrest status and possible prosecution. As Suzanne had left the set when the trouble began, she was not among the detained.

Randy Guswhite sat alone in a corner, the only one with a broad smile on his face. Freddie West lay on a long bench, his mummified, bandage-wrapped arms protruding skyward.

Jack and his cronies hung out in the opposite corner, each appearing both down in the mouth yet, at the same time, looking and acting very much at home.

Daniel stood by the bars at the front and looked hopefully towards an approaching cop. "Randy Guswhite?" the police officer called.

"I know," said Randy, standing up with a delighted grin on his face. "My lawyer's here!"

"How did you know?" asked the police officer, beaten to the punch.

"I have my powers back!" replied Randy, barely able to contain his shameless glee.

"Well, isn't that special?" commented the officer sardonically, as he opened the cell door to let Randy out. "Waterstone?" shouted the officer.

"Yes?" answered Daniel, hopefully.

"You're free to go, too."

Suzanne stood at the police desk. She greeted Daniel as he was guided to sign his release papers. "I had my lawyers secure your release," she informed him. "They don't expect any charges to be filed against you."

"Aren't you angry?" asked Daniel as they turned to leave the station. "All your hard work ended by a single TV broadcast?"

"I'm a survivor, Daniel. Survivors always bounce back. This is yours," she said as she handed him an envelope.

"What is it?" Daniel asked suspiciously.

"Your first book, *Heartache*?"

"Yeah?"

"It got short-listed for the Superior Critics Book Awards. It's selling like hot cakes."

"This check is dated two weeks ago?" Daniel remarked. "You knew this all the time?"

"With everything going on, it must have slipped my mind," Suzanne answered, tongue in cheek.

Daniel pocketed the check and turned to walk in the opposite direction.

"You'll still need the services of a literary agent," Suzanne said and smiled.

"I'll call you," Daniel said, not meaning it. "Take care, Suzanne," he said as he crossed the street.

"You too," she said, not loudly enough for him to hear.

Daniel's demeanor brightened considerably, a broad smile breaking out upon his face when he saw Clare exiting the parking lot. He lit up when he saw that she saw him, and walked quickly and excitedly towards her. "I'm so proud of you!" she exclaimed as she reached out and wrapped her arms tightly around him.

"I love you, too!" Daniel declared, perhaps not hearing

her properly.

"We may be broke but we'll be happy, I know we will," Clare spoke excitedly. "We'll rent some place small, start all over—"

"Clare," interrupted Daniel, as he stroked her hair lovingly with his right hand. "You said you read my first novel, *Heartache*, right?"

"Terrific novel, Daniel. But you'll probably have to lie low for a while, until all this blows over and you can reestablish yourself as a serious writer, again. Maybe we can get you some teaching work; I'm sure you'd be a wonderful teacher. You did the right thing," she said, hugging him tightly again.

Daniel held the check up to her eye line. "*Heartache* is selling," he said.

Checking out the modest yet meaningful royalty payment, Clare took a deep breath and sighed contentedly, as if her brain was shifting gears to a much more desirable and relaxed frame of mind. "You're going to be a much better writer after all of this," she explained. "I can't wait to read what you're going to write next."

"I don't care what I'm writing next," said Daniel, surprising himself with his new thought. "As long as we're together, I really don't care what I write next."

And, as the hurly-burly of rush hour traffic and the hustle of office workers passed them by in a hurry to get home, Daniel and Clare kissed each other so intensely, it was as if they were in a completely different place, a shimmering love-filled time and space, exclusively their own.

EPILOGUE

Contrary to Daniel's assertion, that his TV appearance (exposing the brain book as a work of madness and his admittance that the Brain organization was run by ethically challenged opportunists), had dealt a death blow to the book and to Suzanne's company, the subsequent reality proved to be quite the opposite. Not only had sales of the book not been irreparably damaged, in actual fact, sales of the book sky-rocketed.

Much to the astonishment of just about everyone on the planet, *You Have a Brain—Use it!* in a few short years became the best-selling book of all time, outstripping the next-highest best seller by a factor of at least three. Translated into over two hundred languages, the book's appeal crossed over every national and cultural divide.

Admirers, as well as critics of the book continued to be at a complete loss as to why a book written by a self-confessed crazy person, filled with ideas which he did not believe in, condone or advocate, could not only capture the imagination of hundreds of millions of people but also have such an astonishing effect to the consciousness of the entire human race.

Having read the book, and having performed some or all of the exercises outlined in its pages, hundreds of thousands of people of every hue and nationality across the globe reported an expansion of consciousness. Most of those readers claimed the ability to perform miracles. Many experts in the field of consciousness suggested that what was happening, on an individual level would, at some point, by virtue of critical mass, reach a tipping point and alter the consciousness of humanity, as a whole.

Debates and arguments continued to rage, for years after the date of the book's publication, as to how much an effect the book had upon the expansion of the consciousness of the human race. Yet, most agreed that the book, and the exercises contained therein, had certainly had some kind of mind-expanding effect upon the average reader. This expansion of mind, or alteration of consciousness, had far surpassed the effect of any other book written before or since.

In short, *You Have a Brain—Use it!* not only changed the collective consciousness of the human race but may also have been responsible for changing the direction in which homo sapiens, as a whole began to head, or, at the very least, had effected a sort-of speeding up in mankind's evolution.

Spearheading the success of the book was Suzanne and her organization, Brain, Inc. As all rights and interest in the book had been signed over to her by the author, Suzanne Goldenstock soon became not just the richest but also, arguably, the most powerful person on the planet.

Her rise in wealth and power took an exponential increase when she incorporated the Brain organization as a church and the teachings and philosophy of the brain book, and of their author, Charles Spectrum, as a religion. The Church of Healing and Applied Brain Science (C-HABS) soon became the fastest-growing religious organization on every continent, its assets valued in the tens of billions of US dollars.

After a short stint in jail, Suzanne's brother, Jack would rejoin C-HABS and become head of the Office of Developmental Strategies (ODS), a controversial unit within the church that involved itself with regulating and monitoring "standards and practices" among its members.

So many controversies and allegations of harassment, in particular, surrounded the behavior of the officers of the unit that it became known to many people critical of it methods as the "dirty tricks" department of the church.

Following the failure of Randy Guswhite's next two published books, Randy joined C-HABS initially as a consultant and adviser to the church's many practitioners and ministers but soon moved up the ranks to become a charismatic leader in his own right and head of the Devotional and Charismatic Office of the church.

Freddie West wrote a book about his experiences with Brain, Incorporated and his investigative reporting of the early formation of the church. The book was published by a small vanity press which shortly thereafter was destroyed in a fire along with all copies of the book. Although many conspiracy theories have alleged foul play and connect the fire with the subsequent mysterious disappearance of the author, no such allegations have ever been proved.

Having renounced all claim to and all knowledge of the authorship of the brain book, Daniel Waterstone lived a low-key life with his wife, Clare. His award-nominated book, *Heartache* did not proceed beyond the short-list stage of the awards competition and soon thereafter dropped to the lower end of book sales rankings, joining his other books in print, *All Alone in an Insane World* and *The Impossible Dream: Part One.* Splitting his time between teaching English literature at a local community college and sometimes moonlighting as a Teaching English as a Foreign Language (TEFL) teacher in order to support his non-working wife and growing family, Daniel continued to write books that he considered to be following in the footsteps of the great American authors (and true to the literary masterpieces of what was debatably becoming a bygone age).

In her ever-decreasing spare time, Clare continued to compose music free from the constraints and dictates of the commercial marketplace. Her modern day symphonies, once completed, would invariably be work-shopped and subsequently performed by the amateur orchestra at the community college where her husband taught. Such outings would become a major highlight in the calendar of the creative couple's life.

Loving every minute of his teaching, where he shared his joy of literature with young students (who sadly seemed more intent upon sharing their thoughts and concerns on Twitter and other social networking sites than learning), Daniel nevertheless persevered and accepted whatever gains or defeats he encountered in life with tolerant equanimity.

Ascribing his increasing sense of purpose, acceptance and tolerance to what he perceived as major challenges in his life, to his ever-loving and supportive wife, Daniel continued, over the years, to develop a sense of gratitude and an ever-deepening love the likes of which he had never before known or experienced.

Not only did his wife, Clare, enrich his life with her all-accepting love and generosity, she also was to endow him with four sons and three daughters, all in relatively short order. It was in this new role, as a protective, supportive and loving father and husband, that Daniel would finally discover himself fully and come to understand and deeply appreciate the nature of his own true self and the purpose of the life, which he intimately shared, with what he had once described as "common humanity."

In between teaching, writing, diaper changing, soccer practice, family outings, and the occasional dinner dates with his beautiful wife, Daniel would never know loneliness again.

ABOUT THE AUTHOR

Dermot Davis is an award-winning playwright, having had plays performed in Dublin, Boston and Los Angeles. His creative work encompasses varied genres and styles — drama, comedy, and, more recently, sci-fi, with a special focus on human themes and characters transformed by life experience. A sometimes actor, he is a co-founder of the Laughing Gravy Theatre (which performed Irish Vaudeville and excerpts of Irish literary works as well as drama, including the original stage plays of Mr. Davis) where he and other members of the troupe were artists-in-residence at the Piccolo Spoleto Festival in Charleston, South Carolina. He currently resides in Los Angeles. Follow him on his Goodreads.com Author Page at http://www.goodreads.com/author/show/6565450.Dermot Davis.

OTHER BOOKS BY DERMOT DAVIS

Zen and Sex
Stormy Weather

CPSIA information can be obtained at www.ICGtesting.com
Printed in the USA
LVOW06s1635300114

371669LV00014B/541/P